Goldwhiskers

SPY MICE
Goldwhiskers

HEATHER VOGEL FREDERICK

illustrations by **SALLY WERN COMPORT**

Aladdin Paperbacks

New York > London > Toronto > Sydney

ALADDIN PAPERBACKS
An imprint of Simon & Schuster Children's Publishing Division
1230 Avenue of the Americas, New York, New York 10020
Text copyright © 2007 by Heather Vogel Frederick
Illustrations copyright © 2007 by Sally Wern Comport
All rights reserved, including the right of reproduction
in whole or in part in any form.
ALADDIN PAPERBACKS and colophon are trademarks of
Simon & Schuster, Inc.
Designed by Greg Stadnyk and Jessica Sonkin
The text for this book was set in Stone Serif.
The illustrations for this book were rendered in mixed drawing mediums.
Manufactured in the United States of America
First Aladdin Paperbacks edition January 2007
2 4 6 8 10 9 7 5 3 1
Library of Congress Cataloging-in-Publication Data
Frederick, Heather Vogel.
Goldwhiskers / Heather Vogel Frederick ; illustrations by Sally Wern Comport.—1st ed.
p. cm. (Spy Mice)
Summary: During a London vacation, Oz Levinson must deal with the bullying
Priscilla Winterbottom, while mouse spy Glory Goldenleaf tracks the whereabouts of
a valuable jewel, missing orphaned mouselings, and two evil ministers of rats.
ISBN-13: 978-1-4169-1442-6   ISBN-10: 1-4169-1442-0
[1. Spies—Fiction. 2. Mice—Fiction. 3. Rats—Fiction.]
I. Comport, Sally Wern, ill. II. Title.
PZ7.F87217 Go   [Fic]—dc22 2005034360

For my true-blue sisters Lisa and Stefanie,
with whom I shared a happy childhood interlude in England

CHAPTER 1

**DRY ONE
DECEMBER 23
0001 HOURS**

At exactly one minute past midnight, a large black taxicab turned into the sweeping drive in front of London's Savoy Hotel.

A mouseling stepped out of the shadow of the curb as the vehicle approached. Its headlights caught the hopeful gleam in his bright little eyes. He watched as the cab pulled up smartly in front of the entrance. It swished through a puddle as it did so, drenching him with icy water.

The mouseling slumped back against the curb, the hopeful look instantly extinguished. He'd thought that perhaps his luck had finally changed. It hadn't. Not one bit. He swiped dejectedly at his sodden face with a grimy paw and sneezed. What a horrid night! The skies were spouting the kind of cold, sleeting rain that only London in late December could produce—and now this. His slight body shook violently, and the mouseling wrapped his tail tightly around himself in a vain attempt to keep warm.

Shivering, he watched as the cab driver hopped out and trotted round to open the door for his passengers. The mouseling's tummy rumbled. Not only had he had no luck tonight, he'd had nothing to eat either. He hadn't earned it yet. "Only mouselings who sing for their supper get their supper," Master always said.

And the mouseling desperately wanted to please Master. Master was the giver of all that was good: food, warmth, praise. The mouseling owed Master his life. Before Master, he'd been nothing. An urchin. A throwaway. "Nobody wants worthless street trash like you," Master reminded him often. Reminded all of them often. "Nobody but me."

Still shivering, the mouseling peered over the curb as two pairs of feet emerged from the taxi: a lady's and a gentleman's. His tiny heart began to beat a little faster. Maybe his luck had changed after all. The gentleman's shoes were highly polished and expensive looking. The lady's stylish sandals crisscrossed her pale toes with narrow straps. Useless for walking, especially in this weather, but perfect for making an impressive entrance at one of London's poshest hotels. Which was just the sort of thing that toffs liked to do.

"You can always tell a toff by his shoes," Master had instructed. "That and his bags. Toffs like to spend money on shoes and bags."

The cab driver removed a trio of suitcases from the taxi's trunk and placed them on the sidewalk. The mouseling watched intently. He lifted his grubby little nose into the air and sniffed. Leather! Expensive leather. Hope soared in him once again. This was what he'd been waiting for all evening. These were just the sort of bags that toffs liked to take to fancy hotels.

And toffs—upper-crust, well-heeled, wealthy humans—were what the mouseling was after tonight. What all Master's mouselings were after in every corner of the city tonight.

The small mouse's tummy rumbled again. *Right, then.* Time to get to work if he fancied any supper. He shouldered his soggy duffel bag (made from the toe of a sock) and with a practiced leap swung himself up over the curb. As the taxi-cab pulled away, he tumbled into the cuff of the gentle-man's well-cut trousers, and a moment later the Savoy's doorman ushered the two human guests—and one unseen mouseling—inside the hotel.

CHAPTER 2

DAY ONE
DECEMBER 23
0600 HOURS

The British airport official
looked up from the counter at the
chubby boy standing in front of him.
"Purpose of your visit?" he asked.

The boy, who was sweating pro-
fusely, prodded at the round, wire-rimmed glasses slipping
down his nose. "Uh, I guess, uh—" he stammered, still a bit
groggy from the long flight from Washington, D.C.
Nervous, too. This was his last hurdle. Once he passed
through immigration and customs he was home free.

"Purpose of your visit?" repeated the man. There was a
note of irritation in his voice. Behind the boy, a long line of
waiting travelers snaked through the airport's crowded
screening area. "Business or pleasure?"

"Um," said the boy. A bit of both was the correct
answer, but how many ten-year-olds had business in
London? He didn't want to arouse suspicion. He couldn't
afford to do that. Not with what he had hidden in his shoe.
"Um," he said again.

5

"Are you hard of hearing, lad?" demanded the official, glaring at him. "What's your name, anyway?" He squinted down at the passport that lay open on the counter in front of him. His bushy eyebrows shot up and disappeared beneath the bill of his uniform cap. "Ozymandias Levinson? Blimey, who names a kid Ozymandias?"

A blush eclipsed the boy's round moon of a face. "It's just Oz, actually," he muttered. He glanced anxiously over to where his parents, whose passports had already been approved and stamped, were waiting.

Oz had never seen such a busy airport. Two days before Christmas, Heathrow was a virtual crush of humanity. The corridors and waiting areas were jammed with people of all shapes and sizes and colors from every corner of the world. Europe, Asia, Africa, India. Women in bright saris. Men in business suits and turbans. Students with backpacks; parents with babies in strollers. Old people, young people, all of them squeezing through the checkpoint like soda through the neck of a bottle, eager to pop out the other side and explore the great city of London that lay just beyond the airport's doors.

Oz took a deep breath. He needed to say something, and fast. He needed to say one word: "pleasure." Only problem was, it was a lie. Not completely, but still a lie. And Oz wasn't very good at lying. He got red in the face. He stammered. He broke out in a sweat. Just like he was doing now. *Get a grip, Levinson,* he told himself sternly. *James Bond would lie.*

James Bond was Oz's hero. The British superspy was

always rock steady under pressure. Just like he, Oz Levinson, would be when he was a grown-up secret agent someday. He was sort of a secret agent already—an honorary one, anyway. Only he wasn't very good at it yet.

The airport official tapped the end of his pen against Oz's passport impatiently.

The name is Levinson. Oz Levinson, Oz repeated silently, steeling himself with his favorite mantra. He closed his eyes, opened his mouth, and prepared to lie.

"Excuse me, but are you nearly finished?" said a female voice.

Oz's eyes flew open. He looked up in surprise. Way up. So did the airport official. Oz's mother was standing beside them. At nearly six feet tall, she towered over the seated man. He frowned.

"It's forbidden to return to this checkpoint," he said severely.

Another official in uniform hustled over. He placed a newspaper on the counter and pointed to one of the headlines, then leaned down and whispered something into his colleague's ear. Oz caught the phrase "VIP."

Oz was very familiar with that phrase. His mother was a world-famous opera star who was considered a Very Important Person wherever she went.

The seated man scanned the newspaper headline, then cleared his throat. "Lavinia Levinson?" he said, sitting up a little straighter.

Oz's mother inclined her head regally.

"And this is your son?"

Lavinia Levinson placed a protective hand on Oz's shoulder. The official glanced from one to the other. "Ah, yes," he said. "I can see the resemblance."

Oz reddened. Was he making fun of them? Lots of people did. He and his mother were both blond and both, well, on the large side. This morning, his mother was wearing a dramatic red-cashmere cape. Oz thought she looked a bit like Mrs. Santa Claus. *Who does that make me,* he wondered sourly, *Santa's long-lost son, Jumbo?*

The man smiled broadly at Oz's mother. "The missus is a big fan of yours," he gushed. "Might I trouble you for your autograph? It would be a lovely surprise to tuck in her Christmas stocking."

As Lavinia Levinson signed her name on a slip of paper, the man stamped Oz's passport and waved him on toward customs. Oz trotted over to where his father was standing, next to Oz's friend and classmate Delilah Bean, better known as D. B.

"What took you so long?" Luigi Levinson asked.

"Can't talk now—gotta make a pit stop!" Oz cried, racing past them. He needed to be sure that the secret in his left shoe was still safe.

Oz had not been able to stop thinking about his left shoe since the airplane had taken off last night from Washington. He ran into the men's room and locked himself in a stall. Bending over, he quickly removed the shoe. It was very old-fashioned. Oz thought that it looked like something his grandfather might wear. Or like something from a museum. In fact, it *was* from a museum. The International Spy Museum in Washington, D.C., to be exact. Oz's colleagues had retrieved it (and its mate) just last week. It was the first time the agency had attempted to retrieve something so large. The mission had required a massive team effort. Fortunately, things had gone well. Equally fortunately, the shoes had fit Oz.

Oz turned the shoe upside down gently. "You okay?" he whispered into its heel, grateful that no one could see him. He must look like an idiot.

There was no reply from the shoe. Oz grasped its heel and grunted as he tried to swivel it clockwise. Nothing happened. Oz frowned. He grasped the heel again, more firmly this time, and twisted counterclockwise. Again, nothing. Oz looked down at his feet and chewed his lip. It *was* the left shoe, wasn't it? Could he have gotten mixed-up about something as important as that? His heart started to race as he grappled urgently with the heel. Perspiration dripped down his face, and he prodded anxiously at his glasses again. What if he couldn't get it open? What if there weren't enough airholes? What if—wait! There. The heel budged slightly. A wave of relief washed over him. He had the correct shoe after all—it was just stuck. Oz swiveled the heel with all of his might, and this time it opened, revealing a secret compartment.

"You okay, Glory?" he whispered. "Could you breathe in there?"

The contents of the shoe's secret compartment stirred, and a furry head popped out. "Breathing wasn't a problem," said the small brown creature who emerged, stretching. "Bunsen's airholes worked just fine. There wasn't much room, though. I feel like a pretzel."

Oz inspected her closely. "You don't look like a pretzel."

Glory grinned. "Nope, just a mouse."

Morning Glory Goldenleaf is hardly "just" a mouse, thought Oz, smiling back at her. She was an elite Silver Skateboard agent with Washington, D.C.'s Spy Mice Agency, and his colleague and friend.

"I saved these for you," he said, handing her a bag of airline peanuts.

"Thanks, Oz—you're true-blue," Glory replied, tearing into it hungrily. "By the way, remind me to e-mail Bunsen as soon as we get to the hotel and let him know I'm okay. You know how he worries."

Bunsen Burner, lab-mouse-turned-field-agent, was another colleague—and Glory's sweetheart. He'd been very reluctant to stay behind in Washington, and he'd fussed endlessly over the secret compartment in the shoe, adding extra airholes for safety and soft cotton balls to cushion Glory for the journey.

"I can't believe we're actually here!" Glory exclaimed, nibbling on a peanut. "Just think, Oz—we're in England!"

Oz nodded. Lavinia Levinson's invitation from the Royal Opera to sing a Christmas Eve concert had been a stroke of luck for all of them. The Levinsons had quickly decided to make a family vacation of it, and they'd invited D. B. along to keep Oz company. The Beans had been reluctant at first to part with their daughter over the holidays, but Lavinia Levinson's enthusiasm had finally worn them down.

"Just think how educational it will be!" she'd pointed out. "Plus, you'd be doing us a huge favor. I'll be in rehearsal most of the time, and poor Oz will be bored to tears."

Once Glory heard that Oz and D. B. were heading to London, she had decided to hitch a ride and visit her new friend Squeak Savoy. Squeak was an agent with MICE-6, the British equivalent of the Spy Mice Agency. The two mice had become friends on a recent mission battling Roquefort Dupont, the supreme leader of Washington's rat underworld and Glory's arch enemy. Just last month, in New York, they had soundly defeated Dupont and the other rats of the Global Rodent Roundtable, including London's own Stilton Piccadilly. The rats had last been seen floating out to sea in a hot-air balloon, and they hadn't been heard from since.

Glory's trip to London wasn't just a vacation, though. She had an appointment with Sir Edmund Hazelnut-Cadbury, head of MICE-6. She reached down into the shoe's secret compartment and pulled out her backpack. Made from the thumb of a mitten, it contained her skateboard, a letter to Sir Edmund from her boss, Julius Folger, and a brand-new acquisition from the Spy Museum's collection.

Anglo-American mice relations were strong, and the two agencies freely shared intelligence, gadgets, and mouse-power as they worked to keep their world safe from the likes of Dupont and Piccadilly.

Glory shouldered her backpack. She had high hopes for this visit. A vacation, yes—but possibly a little more than that too. If she played her cards right, Christmas in London could herald the beginning of a glamorous overseas posting. And Glory dearly wanted a glamorous overseas posting.

"We'd better go," said Oz. "They're going to wonder where I disappeared to."

Glory climbed onto Oz's waiting palm. He lifted his hand to his chest, and she somersaulted expertly into the pocket of his shirt. Oz put his shoe back on and went to rejoin his parents and D. B.

"Everything okay?" whispered his classmate as Oz's parents whisked them through customs and outside to the waiting limousine. Oz gave her a thumbs-up and pointed to his shirt pocket.

The limo's smooth, sedate pace quickly lulled Oz's mother to sleep. Her head slumped back against the bearlike arm her husband had draped around her shoulders, and her mouth fell open. The world-famous diva let out a gentle snore. D. B. giggled.

"I still can't believe my parents let me come," she said to Oz, bouncing in her seat. The profusion of tiny braids that covered her head bounced too. "This is so awesome."

Oz stared at his classmate. He'd never seen D. B. this

excited—or this cheerful. This new and improved D. B. was a little unnerving.

As they drew closer to the city, familiar landmarks began to appear.

"Look!" squealed D. B. "There's Big Ben!"

Oz craned his neck for a better view of the enormous clock tower atop the Houses of Parliament. Luigi Levinson smiled. "Excited, kids?"

Oz and D. B. both nodded.

"We'll get some breakfast at the hotel, then go exploring," Oz's father promised. "I think the folks at the Royal Opera have some kind of tour planned for us while your mother is in rehearsal."

"I can't wait to see the Crown Jewels!" said D. B. "Do you think we could go there first?"

Oz grunted. D. B. hadn't shut up about the Crown Jewels since leaving Washington. "What's so special about a bunch of jewelry?"

D. B. gaped at him. "Oz, this is hardly 'a bunch of jewelry,'" she snapped, sounding much more like her usual self. She flipped open a guidebook and thrust it under his nose. "We're talking crowns worn by centuries of kings and queens here. We're talking diamonds and sapphires and rubies bigger than you-know-who." She gave a significant nod toward the small lump nestled in Oz's shirt pocket. "Plus, they're kept in the Tower of London, where they used to chop people's heads off."

Oz shrugged. "I guess I wouldn't mind seeing that," he

said grudgingly. Personally, he was looking forward to the James Bond walking tour. He'd read about it in one of his mother's guidebooks. London was Agent 007's home base.

Crown jewels, castles, walking tours—whatever they did, London was going to be great, Oz thought happily. After all, London was three thousand miles away from Washington, D.C., and Chester B. Arthur Elementary School. London was three thousand miles away from the sharks.

That's what Oz called the bullies at his school—including Jordan Scott and Sherman "Tank" Wilson, a pair of sixth graders who lived to torment younger and weaker kids like himself. And now he'd left them far, far behind.

A whole week without sharks! Oz settled back into his seat with a smile. It was almost too good to be true.

CHAPTER 3

DAY ONE
DECEMBER 23
0600 HOURS

"I never want to see another
herring as long as I live," snarled
Roquefort Dupont, poking his long,
ugly snout over the edge of the
wharf and heaving himself up onto its
weather-beaten planks. In one of his filthy paws, the
supreme leader of Washington, D.C.'s rat underworld—and
recently elected Big Cheese of the Global Rodent
Roundtable—clutched a makeshift leash. He yanked on it,
dragging a scrawny, bedraggled mouse up onto the dock
beside him. "Don't you agree, Fumble?"

The mouse nodded listlessly. He looked miserable, and
he reeked of fish. They both reeked of fish. They'd had
nothing but herring to eat since a freak storm had blown
them off course and the balloon on which they'd been
traveling had crash-landed in the North Sea.

Dupont's Parisian cousin, Brie de Sorbonne, leaped
nimbly up beside them. *"Moi aussi,"* she said with a delicate
shudder. *"Au revoir* to herring!" She looked back in distaste

at the Norwegian fishing trawler anchored behind them, then glanced at a gleaming white cruise ship docked several wharves away. "Such a pity we weren't picked up by one of zose," she added ruefully. "Now, zat's ze way to travel."

"After that storm, we were lucky we got picked up at all," grunted a broad-shouldered rat who was clambering onto the dock beside her. It was Stilton Piccadilly, head of London's rat forces. Behind him, the other members of the Global Rodent Roundtable hauled themselves up the rope that tethered the fishing boat to the wharf in Oslo's harbor. The rats huddled together in the chilly predawn air, their stomachs sending up a loud chorus of hungry rumbles.

Piccadilly was right. Without the *Dagmar Elisabeth* and her captain's sharp eyes, the entire G.R.R. would be at the bottom of the sea right now instead of standing on a dock in Norway. Lucky for them, the trawler's skipper had spotted their bright balloon afloat on the water and angled closer for a better look. He'd quickly recognized it as the replica of the Pilgrim ship *Mayflower* that had escaped from the Macy's Thanksgiving Day Parade in New York City. The fiasco had made headlines worldwide. Grappling the balloon up onto the deck, the captain had stored it away in the ship's hold, intending to mail it back to its owner as soon as he reached port. The rats, hidden in the balloon's deflated folds, had been stored along with it. They'd remained trapped aboard the *Dagmar Elisabeth* for weeks as the ship poked its way through Norway's fjords and inlets, slowly filling her cargo bays with herring.

Brie caught sight of her reflection in the window of a nearby warehouse and shrieked. Her companions whirled around, fangs bared and claws at the ready.

"What! Where?" snarled Dupont, primed for a fight.

Brie covered her eyes with her paws and pointed wordlessly at the window with her tail. The other rats gasped as they, too, spotted themselves.

"I'm a walking skeleton!" cried Dupont, aghast. He poked his prominent ribs in dismay.

"Skin *und* bones, *ja*," agreed Muenster Alexanderplatz. The big, black rat from Berlin, better known as Muenster the Monster, plucked sadly at his own gaunt hide.

It was true. The rats were an exceedingly skinny lot, thanks to the trawler's all-herring-and-nothing-but-herring diet.

Gorgonzola, the senior rodent in the group, stepped forward. His belly, though still ample, no longer scraped the ground as he walked. "Food," demanded the Italian rat, "*pronto*. Then home. For me, *Roma*!"

Everyone stared at Dupont expectantly. As Big Cheese, he was in charge of this sort of thing. Never one to miss an opportunity to pass the buck, however, Dupont swung around and glared at Ridder Stortinget. "This is your neighborhood, right? Where do we eat?"

The Norwegian rat jerked his snout away from the harbor. "My lair is close," he replied. "Come, I show you."

Stortinget scuttled away in the early morning darkness, and the herd of rats scuttled after him. Stilton Piccadilly,

Brie, and Roquefort Dupont—still dragging the pitiful heap of fur that was Fumble—brought up the rear.

When they reached the subway station where the Norwegian rat had his headquarters, the G.R.R. quickly scattered in search of food and transportation home.

"In a few hours I will be in Paris," gloated Brie. "A bubble bath first, and then fresh croissants, *oui*?" She gave a contented sigh and glanced over at Dupont. "Won't you change your mind and come with me, *mon cousin*?"

"Some other time," said Dupont. "I have to get back to D.C." Roquefort Dupont was worried about his turf. He'd been gone for nearly a month now, and he was all too aware of what havoc his underlings could be wreaking in his absence. Gnaw, one of his senior aides-de-camp, had tried to take over once before, and Dupont wouldn't put it past the one-eared slimeball to try again.

Brie leaned over and kissed both of Dupont's furry cheeks. "*Au revoir*, zen," she whispered silkily. "Until we meet again. Perhaps you will consider holding ze next Roundtable meeting in Paris? April would be *très bien*. Nothing is lovelier zan springtime in ze City of Lights."

Tossing a wink at Stilton Piccadilly, who blushed an unattractive shade of crimson, Brie sashayed off into the subway station's shadows. Dupont tugged on Fumble's leash. "Let's go."

"Wait," ordered Stilton Piccadilly.

Dupont halted. He eyed the British rat suspiciously. Piccadilly pointed to a bundle of newspapers. "Look," he said.

The G.R.R.'s extended voyage to Europe had reaped them one benefit. Bored to distraction on the trawler, the rats had discovered a stack of international newspapers and finally allowed Dupont—with Fumble's help—to teach them to read.

"The London *Times,* eh?" said Dupont, squinting at the masthead. He scanned the front page. "'World-Famous Opera Star to Sing in London on Christmas Eve!'" he read aloud. His tail began to whip back and forth as he inspected the photo beneath the headline. "It's her, isn't it?"

Piccadilly nodded.

With his razor-sharp teeth, Dupont snipped the twine that bound the papers. He dragged the top copy into the shadows and nosed through the pages in search of the rest of the article. "'Lavinia Levinson arrives in London today, accompanied by her family,'" Dupont muttered. Stilton Piccadilly read along over his shoulder. "'The diva will sing a program of seasonal favorites at the Royal Opera House on Christmas Eve. An exclusive reception will follow. In attendance will be members of the royal family, along with a glittering gathering of film stars and other celebrities.'"

Dupont gave another sharp tug on Fumble's leash. The mouse flinched. "Yessir?" he mumbled, rising onto his paws.

With all of his usual henchrodents far away in Washington, D.C., the Sewer Lord had needed a replacement underling to do his bidding. Fumble, a former employee of the Spy Mice Agency who had turned traitor, was it now. He served as Roquefort Dupont's personal slave.

Dupont tapped the paper with his scaly tail. "What does that mean exactly, 'accompanied by her family'?" he demanded.

Fumble shrugged. "Husband and son."

"You sure about that?"

"Oz is an only child," explained the mouse. "If he weren't traveling with them, the article would have just said 'accompanied by her husband.'" He slumped back to the floor.

Dupont stared at the newspaper. Then he looked up. He gave Stilton Piccadilly a calculating stare.

"I know exactly what you're thinking, Dupont," growled the British rat. "I can read you like a book."

Roquefort Dupont's thin rat lips peeled back in a hideous smile. "I told you reading would come in handy," he said smugly.

Piccadilly glared at him. "Listen, you pompous piece of sewer sludge. Let me make one thing absolutely clear. I don't like you. Not one bit. In fact, I loathe you."

"I can assure you that the feeling is mutual," snarled Dupont. The two bull rats squared off, the hackles of fur around their grimy necks bristling in anger. "You despise me, yes," Dupont continued, "but I suspect that, for once, you agree with me."

Piccadilly was silent for a long moment. Then he nodded reluctantly.

"And you'll help?" asked Dupont.

The British rodent eyed him. "What's in it for me?"

Dupont gave a short bark of laughter. "Greedy beggar," he said. "I might have guessed there'd be a price." He paused, considering. "Second-in-command of the Global Rodent Roundtable," he said finally.

"Deal," snapped Stilton Piccadilly. He extended his hairless tail.

With a grimace of distaste, Dupont extended his own as well, and the two rats shook in a formal truce. Then Dupont jerked on the leash again, yanking Fumble onto his paws.

"Let's get a move on," he said. "Washington can wait. We've got some unfinished business to take care of in London."

CHAPTER 4

DAY ONE
DECEMBER 23
0800 HOURS

High atop a building overlooking
the Thames, a shaft of weak winter sunlight nudged its way through a crack in
the largest clock face in London. Most
tourists would have been surprised to dis-
cover that this honor fell not to Big Ben, but rather to a clock
farther downriver atop a building beside the Savoy Hotel. The
feeble ray slipped in beside the enormous minute hand just as
it swept the top of the hour, unfurling across the floor of the
darkened cubbyhole hidden behind it. The sunbeam came to
rest on a tightly curled ball of fur in the far corner.

Twist stirred in his sleep. The scraps of flannel in his nest
were warm, and he burrowed more deeply into them, squinch-
ing his eyes tight against the encroaching daylight. He'd been
out until very late last night, and he was still very tired.

"Rise and shine, mouselings!"

Reluctantly, Twist opened one eye. Master was calling,
and when Master called, mouselings obeyed. He blinked
sleepily, then stretched and yawned. All around him, in the

nests lining the room's remotest corner, other mouselings did the same.

"Morning chores first!"

Twist climbed obediently out of his nest. He tidied it quickly, gave his furry face a quick splash in the nearby basin (a gold-rimmed china egg cup), then shuffled over to help two other mouselings open the cubbyhole's bank of windows.

The morning air was bracingly cold, but the rain had stopped, and the broad river below sparkled in the sunlight. Even at this early hour, barges and tourist boats plowed its murky waters, some furrowing their way downriver toward the Tower of London, others heading in the opposite direction toward Big Ben. Across the Thames stood the London Eye, the gigantic Ferris wheel that was one of the city's newest landmarks. Twist regarded it curiously. *What would it be like to ride the wheel up, up, up into the sky?* he wondered.

"Finish up, mouselings, then gather round!"

Twist scurried to join the other mice as they completed their chores, taking his place alongside the rope that serviced the dumbwaiter. The sun was stronger now, and as it poured through the windows, it revealed the cubbyhole to be not a bleak, cheerless space, but something more along the lines of Ali Baba's cave. The battered floorboards were layered thickly with bright oriental carpets; the walls were hung with lengths of rich silk brocade heavily fringed in gold. At one end of the room a cheery fire blazed behind an ornate brass grate. Beside the fireplace stood a handsome red-leather chair. In the chair sat the one the mouselings called Master.

Twist avoided looking at him. He focused instead on the task at hand, and on the mice nearby who were tidying Master's grand bed, smoothing its linen sheets and fluffing its down coverlet and many pillows. Even after all these weeks, being in Master's presence still inspired feelings of awe in Twist. Fear, too.

"Pull, lads!" called the brawny mouseling at the head of the rope. "Put your backs into it!"

Twist grunted and heaved with the others as they swayed a large basket up through a trapdoor in the floorboards. The scent of something delicious wafted out from under a napkin-covered platter inside, and Twist's tummy rumbled. Master's breakfast. He hoped that there would be something left over for them. When, what, and how much they ate—or if they ate at all—depended entirely on Master's mood and whims. There were plenty of times when Twist and the other mouselings had displeased Master and gone hungry as a result. Twist helped secure the basket, then assembled with the other mouselings in front of the red-leather chair. Gathering his courage, he looked up. Seated in the chair was a gray rat. A huge gray rat. The most enormous rat, in fact, that Twist had ever seen.

"I have a treat for you this morning," Master announced.

Twist, who hadn't realized he'd been holding his breath, exhaled in relief. Master was in a good mood! He could hear it in his voice. Life was always so much easier when Master was in a good mood.

Twist watched as Dodge, Master's most trusted mouseling, finished applying the gold nail polish that she brushed

on Master's whiskers every morning. Long and bristling, they glittered in the morning sunlight. Dodge puffed on them briefly to set the finish, then returned the brush to its trial-sized vial, which she placed carefully in a gold-lacquered box on the table beside the red-leather chair.

"One of you did well last night," said the rat. "Very well. And you know Master's rule: 'When one mouseling surprises, all mouselings get prizes.'" His voice was deep and melodious. It was a soothing voice. Hypnotic, almost. The tight, anxious places inside Twist relaxed when he heard Master's voice. It made him feel safe. Not like he'd felt when he was living on the streets.

"This morning's prize is something special for breakfast. And what do you say to that?" The big rat cupped a paw expectantly behind the colossal flap of gray fur that was his ear.

"We thank you kindly, Master, giver of all that is good," the mice chanted obediently in response.

The rat nodded, pleased. He scanned the crowd of mice that stood before him. "Twist, where are you?"

The mouseling's tiny heart skipped a beat at the sound of his name. "Here, sir!" he squeaked.

The rat motioned him forward with a wave of a mani-cured paw. Twist stepped timidly onto the soft carpet, his hind paws swallowed up completely by its deep pile. He approached the chair and bobbed his head in respect.

"Barely a month on the job, this one, and already one of Master's top performers," said the rat. His voice brimmed with approval, and Twist felt a wave of warmth creep over him from the tip of his tail to the tips of his tiny ears. He'd never been singled out before. Not like this, anyway. He'd been singled out plenty of times for punishment, especially in the beginning. But never for praise.

The big rat waved his paw again, and Dodge reached into the box on the table. She pulled out a velvet pouch and handed it to him. The rat extracted a heavy sapphire earring and held it up in the sunlight, turning it this way and that. The precious stone gleamed as blue as the faraway sea.

"Fetched us a good haul of sparklies last night, did our young Twist," said the rat. He eyed the other mouselings. "More than some of you rubbishy orphans fetch in a week. This clever one found himself a pair of toffs, he did." He fished out the earring's mate, along with a diamond necklace and a sapphire-and-diamond ring, which he slipped over one of his gigantic paws. He sat there for a moment, admiring it. "Haven't seen the likes of this since . . . well, since Dodge herself was on the job. Isn't that right, Dodge?"

Dodge gave a saucy flip of her tail and smiled, but she didn't reply. She was a mouse of few words.

"This is what Master wants!" the big rat cried, his voice rising sharply. The assembled mice drew back in alarm. He shook the jewels at them. "Sparklies! Not that useless trash most of you bring me! Master needs sparklies! Master needs—what is it those appalling Yanks call it? Master needs *bling!*" The big rat heaved himself off the chair. He towered over his small band of jewel thieves, glaring. Twist gulped and shrank back. "And why does Master need sparklies?" the rat snarled, leaning down toward them. "Master needs sparklies because of *you*! Because it costs *money* to raise ungrateful ragamuffins! Worthless orphan mouselings nobody else *wants*!"

The big rat took a step forward, and every tail in the room quivered with fear. He stared at the mouselings, his gaze penetrating, hypnotic. "Don't you remember what it's like to be unwanted?" he continued, his voice dropping to a resonant whisper. "To be out on the streets, alone? With no one to take care of you? No one to feed you?"

The mice nodded, their bright little eyes fixed on his glowing red ones.

"Don't you want to please Master? Master who loves you, who keeps you safe?"

"Master, giver of all that is good," chanted the mice automatically.

The big rat nodded in approval. "That's right," he said. "That's what Master wants to hear." He sat down again, and his gaze fell on Twist. His glare softened. "Mouselings like this one know how to please Master!" Once again he held up Twist's haul from the evening before. "These sparklies will fetch Master a pretty price. Well done, Twist."

The rat waved his glittering paw again, and Dodge scampered nimbly over to the breakfast basket. She whisked the napkin off the platter inside, releasing a tantalizing smell into the cubbyhole.

"Buttered crumpets and strawberry jam!" cried the big rat, and the mice cheered.

Dodge motioned to a trio of sturdy mouselings who rushed over and lifted up one of the two thermoses in the basket. As they tipped it forward, Dodge flipped the spout open and poured out a thimble of hot cocoa. She passed it to Twist, along with a hefty chunk of buttered crumpet.

"The rest of you lot line up in an orderly fashion," commanded the big rat as the mouselings crowded forward. "Line up for Master's bounty."

"Master, giver of all that is good!" chanted the mice again.

"What about Farthing?" cried a voice from the back of the throng.

The big rat looked up sharply. "Who said that?" The mice froze. There was a shuffling of paws, but no one replied.

"Worried about our little prisoner, are you?" The rat stroked his glittering whiskers. "Well, I suppose the rascal has had enough punishment for the moment." He clapped his paws together. "Open the oubliette!"

A mouseling scampered obediently to the far end of the cubbyhole, lifted up a corner of the carpet, and flung open a small door in the floorboards beneath. He reached down and hauled a teeny mouseling out of the crevice that the door concealed.

"Farthing!" whispered Twist, as the wee heap of fur was deposited onto the carpet beside him. "Are you all right?"

Farthing merely sniffled in reply. He was the youngest

of the mouselings and had been brought in from an orphan raid by mistake. Too little to be useful, too young to be properly trained, he'd nevertheless caught the big rat's fancy and been kept on as a pet. A naughty pet, as it turned out, whose antics frequently resulted in the ultimate punishment: banishment to the oubliette.

The mere mention of the word sent the mouselings racing for cover. A sunless, airless hole, the oubliette was one of Master's most terrifying punishments.

Twist slipped a bite of crumpet to Farthing and took another sip from his thimble. He gave a start, nearly choking on his cocoa, as the big rat announced, "Twist may do the honors this morning."

Twist's heart began to pound like a tiny jackhammer. He was being asked to serve breakfast to Master! He wiped the crumbs from his whiskers with the back of his paw and crossed to where Dodge was waiting. He'd never been given this honor—or this responsibility—before! Usually it went to one of the older, more experienced mouselings. Motioning to the trio of mice behind her to tilt the second thermos, Dodge carefully guided another stream of steaming liquid into a miniature china cup. She placed it on a small tray, along with a crumpet, and passed the tray to Twist. Frowning in concentration, the mouseling carried it ever so carefully to the red-leather chair. It wouldn't do to spill on Master's prized carpet. He'd seen what happened to those who spilled on Master's prized carpet. He had no desire to spend the day in the oubliette.

"Ah, nothing like a latte first thing in the morning," said the big rat, taking a sip from the offered cup and biting into his crumpet. "The Savoy does do a nice breakfast, if I say so myself. Paper, please."

Twist scampered back to the basket and returned bearing the front page of the *Times*. He smoothed it carefully on the floor in front of the leather chair. The big rat scanned the morning's headlines. He smiled, and his golden whiskers shimmered again in the sunlight. "There we are. Made page one again. Lovely. 'Notorious Cat Burglar Strikes Again—London's Poshest Hotels on Full Alert for the Holidays.'" He chuckled to himself and took another sip of coffee. "'Cat burglar,' eh? Little do they know. 'Rat burglar' is more like it. With a bit of help from you lot, of course," he added, nodding at the ranks of orphan mice munching contentedly before him. "Would you mouselings like to know a secret?"

The mice stopped chewing. They nodded, their bright little eyes alight with interest.

"Very well then, you shall hear a secret," said the rat. He leaned down closer to his band of diminutive pickpockets. "It's not only our fair city's hotels that need to be on full alert," he whispered conspiratorially. "Not at all. Master has bigger fish to fry. Much bigger fish. Bigger even than any of those pea-brained humans can imagine." He placed a bejeweled paw on Twist's thin shoulder. "And with this clever chap, Master may have finally found a way to carry it off."

CHAPTER 5

DAY ONE
DECEMBER 23
0900 HOURS

"Prudence! How lovely to see you again!"

Oz watched as his mother sailed across the lobby of the Savoy, her red wool cape flapping behind her. A woman Oz had never seen before sailed back toward her. The two met in the middle of the hotel lobby like a pair of cruise ships and exchanged air kisses and thin smiles.

"Lavinia, darling! It's been ages," replied the woman called Prudence. She was rather fierce looking, Oz observed, with a long, thin, pointed nose and sharp dark eyes. In fact, thought Oz, she looked like a ferret. His eyes traveled to the pouf of brown curls that crouched atop her head. A ferret having a bad hair day.

Oz's mother motioned him forward, along with his father and D. B. "I'd like you meet my family," she said. "Prudence Winterbottom, this is my husband, Luigi."

"Enchanted," Oz's father said, clasping Prudence

Winterbottom's hand in his own two bearlike paws. "Your recent recording of *Tosca*—well, what is there to say?"

Oz gave his father a sidelong glance. His father had had plenty to say about Prudence Winterbottom's *Tosca*, none of it very nice. His father was being polite. But Prudence Winterbottom, who wasn't aware of this, preened at what she assumed was praise.

"And this is my son, Ozymandias," continued Lavinia Levinson. "And Oz's best friend, Delilah Bean."

"D. B.," muttered D. B. ungraciously.

Prudence Winterbottom inclined her brown ferret curls at the two of them. "Delighted, I'm sure," she said vaguely. She turned back to Oz's father. "Tell me more about *Tosca*. Did you really like it?"

"Funny, she doesn't look delighted," whispered D. B. to Oz.

"She's a soprano too," Oz whispered back. "With the Royal Opera. They can be kind of, um, touchy."

"Are she and your mom rivals?"

Oz shrugged. "Maybe," he replied. "Yeah, I guess."

"And who do we have here?" boomed Luigi Levinson. "Is this your little snickerdoodle I've heard so much about?"

Oz rolled his eyes at D. B., who smiled. Oz's father was always calling people embarrassing names like "snicker-doodle" and "sugarplum."

"Snickerdoodle?" The British soprano stared blankly at Luigi Levinson. "Ah, you mean my daughter." She reached back and drew forward the girl who was hiding behind her. "Say good morning, Priscilla."

"Good morning, Priscilla," said Priscilla smartly.

Her mother's grip on her shoulder tightened. "Well," she said brightly. "Shall we get started? Busy day ahead. Nigel is waiting in the limousine."

As he was herded through the doors of the Savoy, Oz inspected the two Winterbottoms with growing alarm. Priscilla's mother looked like a ferret, and Priscilla looked just like her mother. This was the girl his parents had told him about at breakfast? The one he and D. B. were expected to spend the day with while his mother was in rehearsal? The one who was to join them on the tour of London that the Royal Opera had arranged? Priscilla Winterbottom did not look like the sort of person who would want to take the James Bond walking tour. In fact, Oz thought unhappily, she looked like—

"Here we are," announced Prudence Winterbottom as they arrived at the limousine that stood waiting for them outside the Savoy. "Come along out, Nigel, and say hello." She leaned in and extracted a short, slender, pale boy who looked to be about eight years old.

"Check out the shorts," Oz whispered to D. B. "Doesn't he know it's almost Christmas?"

The boy named Nigel was indeed dressed in gray flannel shorts. They were hiked up nearly to his armpits, and in addition he wore a blue shirt, a gray flannel jacket, and a red-and-blue-striped tie. On his head was a gray flannel cap. On his legs, gray socks had slipped down to reveal a pair of pale, knobby knees.

"Dude," D. B. replied. "He wouldn't stand a chance with Jordan and Tank."

Oz nodded in sad agreement. "Total shark bait."

"This is Nigel Henshaw," said the British soprano. "Our conductor's son."

"Skipping school, are you?" boomed Luigi Levinson.

Nigel jumped, startled. Oz's father clapped him on his scrawny shoulder reassuringly. "Just kidding, son. I'm glad your father decided to let you come with us. I'm sure we're in for a wonderful day."

Oz saw Nigel give Priscilla Winterbottom a wary glance. *Uh-oh*, he thought as they all climbed into the limousine. He'd seen that look before. Frequently. On his own face. It was a look that said, *I'm a pathetic loser, would you like to kick me?*

"First stop, the Royal Opera House!" trilled Prudence Winterbottom.

The plan was to drop off the two sopranos, then head off to explore London. Oz looked down at the agenda that the limousine driver had given them. He frowned. There was no mention of the James Bond walking tour.

"Laid any eggs today, *Hen*shaw?" Priscilla Winterbottom said under her breath as the grown-ups launched into more discussion of *Tosca*.

A miserable look crept over the younger boy's face. It was another look Oz knew well. Obviously, Nigel had heard this line before.

"Leave the kid alone," snapped D. B.

Priscilla Winterbottom glared at her. She glanced over

35

toward the adults, who were still deep in conversation, then reached out and grabbed one of the braids that covered D. B.'s head like tiny brown springs.

"What's up with your hair?" she demanded, giving it a sharp tug.

"What's up with your mouth?" retorted D. B., swatting Priscilla's hand away.

Priscilla Winterbottom sniffed. She glared at D. B. again, then turned her attention to Oz. She bared her ferret fangs at him in a smile. Staring pointedly at Oz's round belly, Priscilla Winterbottom jerked her chin toward his mother's matching one. "So, are you a soprano as well, then, *Ozymandias?*"

Oz turned beet red. Perspiration broke out on his forehead. His stomach plummeted toward his toes. *Oh, no,* he thought helplessly. There were sharks in England, too.

It was going to be a long week.

CHAPTER 6

DAY ONE
DECEMBER 23
0930 HOURS

Glory gazed down at the mahogany desk in front of her. It was a beautiful piece of furniture, obviously a genuine antique. *Probably foraged from some aristocratic family's dollhouse centuries ago,* she thought, with a tiny pang of homesickness. Her brother Chip, one of the Spy Mice Agency's top foragers, would give his whiskers for a find like this.

The desk was polished to a high gloss, and Glory could see her face reflected in its surface. She looked nervous. She *was* nervous. She shifted uneasily on the cork atop which she perched. Sir Edmund Hazelnut-Cadbury, head of Britain's MICE-6, was seated across the desk from her. He was every bit as imposing as she had expected, and he'd been staring at her in silence for a full three minutes.

Like Julius Folger, her boss back in D.C., Sir Edmund had fur that was silver with age. Like Julius, he wore a bow tie. And like Julius, Sir Edmund had the same dignified bearing befitting a mouse elder. But where Julius's eyes twinkled frequently, Sir Edmund's gaze was somber. At the moment, at least.

The head of MICE-6 cleared his throat. He rattled the file folder in front of him. "So you are Morning Glory Goldenleaf," he said finally.

"Yes, sir," Glory replied, trying to keep her voice level. *Stay calm,* she told herself. *Don't blow this interview.*

"I've heard a great deal about you," said Sir Edmund.

Glory nodded cautiously, unsure how else to respond.

"Most of it positive," continued Sir Edmund.

Most of it? Glory's pulse quickened. She was eager to make a good impression, and "most of it" didn't sound too promising.

"Westminster and Savoy, two of my top agents, both speak very highly of you. And my old friend Julius Folger thinks . . ." He paused and gazed down at the letter that Glory had brought along from her boss.

Curiosity flared in Glory. What exactly *did* Julius think of her? She angled her head slightly, trying to read her boss's familiar scrawl on the Spy Mice Agency's letterhead.

The head of MICE-6 snapped the file shut. "Let's just say you come highly recommended. I, however, have reservations. It states here you were awarded Silver Skateboard status after your very first mission—that disastrous affair with the Kiss of Death."

Glory felt a blush creep across her face. "But it turned out alright in the end," she protested weakly.

Sir Edmund held up a paw, silencing her. "Simply not

the way we do things over here," he told her, shaking his head. "We have different standards altogether."

There was an awkward silence. Sir Edmund cleared his throat. He pushed a platter across the desk. A slightly chipped china saucer, it was stamped with a picture of a red double-decker bus and had clearly been foraged from a rubbish bin behind one of London's many souvenir shops. "Almond?" he offered.

"No, thank you," Glory replied politely. She was still stuffed from breakfast. Squeak's parents ran the Townmouse Grill at the Savoy, a fancy restaurant atop the plaster ceiling of the hotel's Thames Foyer. Upon her arrival earlier this morning, she and Squeak's family had feasted on buttered crumpets with strawberry jam and what seemed like endless pots of tea. Afterward, Glory had settled into the guest nest in Squeak's equally fancy penthouse apartment, tucked under the eaves of the hotel's top floor. It had a fabulous view of the river, and Glory, who still couldn't believe she was actually in London, had had to pry herself away. She'd almost missed her Pigeon Air taxi to the Cabinet War Rooms, where MICE-6 had its headquarters deep beneath Winston Churchill's old wartime bunker.

"Let's get down to business, then," said Sir Edmund, shoving aside the file folder and the platter of almonds. "First things first. Julius informs me that you've brought along a new acquisition from the museum."

Glory opened her backpack and pulled out a silver coin. She handed it to Sir Edmund. He turned it over in his paws, then pressed down on one edge.

"Splendid," he said as the coin flipped open, revealing a hollow interior. "This will prove very useful. Perfect way for our couriers to carry secret messages."

Sir Edmund pushed a button on his intercom. "Miss Honeyberry?" he barked. "Send in agents Westminster and Savoy."

"They're down below at the underground skate park, sir," a soft voice replied. "Finch is showing them a new move. Something about a stale fish, I believe they said?"

"Stale fish 720," noted Glory. "Or 540. Classic Tony Hawk tricks."

"I don't care if the fish is stale or fresh," said Sir Edmund irritably. "Fetch them back at once, and tell them to take the Tube. I haven't got all day."

"Yes, sir."

The intercom went silent. Sir Edmund Hazelnut-Cadbury drummed his tail impatiently on his desk. He opened Glory's folder again and scanned its contents. Glory gazed at the portraits of dignified mice that lined the walls. Sir Edmund's predecessors, apparently: Sir Peregrine Inkwell. Sir Rupert McVitie. Sir Archibald Leach.

Surprisingly, there was a portrait of a human, as well. (A framed postage stamp, actually.) Glory stared at it. She'd seen that face before. The man looked a bit like a bulldog. A very distinguished bulldog.

Sir Edmund looked up from the folder. "Winston Churchill," he said, noting her gaze. "Personal friend of my great-grandfather." He nodded toward the portrait of Sir

Peregrine Inkwell. "Peregrine was my mother's grandfather. Belonged to the Poetry Guild, as did all the Inkwells. He founded MICE-Six."

Sir Edmund leaned forward. "Poets make excellent spies, oddly enough," he informed Glory. "They're clever at reading between the lines, of course, and nothing escapes a poet's keen eye for detail." He pushed back off his cork and stepped closer to the portraits. "They met right here, you know, Churchill and my grandfather," he continued. "Churchill was prime minister during World War II. It was a very dark time. London was under constant attack. Bombs were dropping everywhere. This building served as Churchill's bunker, his secret wartime headquarters."

The elder mouse glanced over at Glory. Her bright little eyes shone with keen interest. She'd learned about Winston Churchill in spy school, but this was different. Sir Edmund was related to a mouse who actually knew him!

"The Blitz affected humans and mice alike," the head of MICE-6 explained. "The bombs threw everything into chaos. The rats of London used it as an excuse to launch a major offensive: the Great Turf War. As luck would have it, my great-grandfather chose to set up our espionage head-quarters in this building, right here beneath Churchill's office." He pointed a paw toward the ceiling. "One night, Peregrine crept upstairs to borrow some ink for a speech he was working on to rally the guilds in his weekly radio address. Perhaps you've heard of it? His famous 'Blood, Tails, Tears, and Sweat' speech?"

Glory nodded. The speech, broadcast over MBC (Mouse Broadcasting Corporation), was one of the most famous and stirring in all of mouse history.

"Great-grandfather was in a hurry to finish in time for the evening broadcast, and he accidentally left a copy on Churchill's desk. The prime minister found it, read it, and left a note in response, expressing his admiration. They began to correspond, exchanging ideas for speeches and encouraging each other in their respective battles against the forces of evil. Rats come in two-legged varieties as well as four, you know."

Glory thought of Jordan and Tank back in Washington, D.C., and nodded in agreement.

"At any rate," continued Sir Edmund, sitting down again, "my great-grandfather finally decided to introduce himself. Only time in our country's history that the Mouse Code has been broken."

Sir Edmund harrumphed and frowned at Glory. She dropped her gaze and inspected the top of the desk again. She knew that Sir Edmund did not approve of her breaking the Mouse Code. Julius had told her so. The head of MICE-6 was worried that teaming up with humans—especially human children—would only lead to disaster.

Sir Edmund opened a small box that lay on the desk in front of him, took out a tiny gold key, and unlocked his bottom desk drawer. He removed something from it and passed it to Glory. "Only photograph in existence of the two of them together," he said.

Glory took the picture in her paws and stared at it. Winston Churchill was seated at his desk, atop which stood Peregrine Inkwell. The two of them stared proudly at the camera. Sir Peregrine was holding something aloft.

"What's that?" asked Glory, trying to make it out.

"Ah," said the head of MICE-6. He reached into the drawer again and pulled out a small silver medallion. He slid it across the desk to Glory. A likeness of Churchill was stamped on its gleaming surface, along with the words NEVER GIVE IN!

"Churchill had this crafted by a silversmith as a gift," said Sir Edmund. "He presented it to my great-grandfather after the war, as a tribute to their triumphs and a reminder of all that they had been through together."

"What does that mean, 'Never give in'?" Glory asked.

"That's a line from one of Churchill's best speeches," explained Sir Edmund. "'Never give in,' he said, 'never give in, *never, never, never, never*—in nothing, great or small, large or petty—never give in except to convictions of honour and good sense.'"

Glory flipped the medallion over. Sir Peregrine Inkwell's noble profile was etched into the other side, along with the words LUX TENEBRAS EXSTINGUIT.

"That's Latin, right?" she said.

Sir Edmund nodded. "It means 'light extinguishes darkness.' Our agency's motto, and a constant reminder that evil always, always falls to the forces of good. Not without a struggle, mind you—sometimes a mighty one. But it always has, and it always will."

Sir Edmund's voice rang with confidence, and he suddenly reminded Glory very much of Julius. She could see why the two were friends.

There was a loud *whirrr!* behind Glory. Startled, she dropped the medallion and swiveled around just in time to see a narrow plastic tube shoot with a *thwump* through a pipe in the wall. It skidded across the carpet and came to a stop beside her. A hatch on the top popped open.

"I believe you are acquainted with Bartholomew Westminster and Squeak Savoy," said Sir Edmund as Glory's friends climbed out.

"Bartholomew?" Glory looked at her colleague in surprise.

Bubble shrugged sheepishly. "Bubble is just my nickname. A few of the lads gave it to me at spy school when I was teamed up with Squeak."

"Stuff and nonsense," said Sir Edmund. "Bartholomew is a perfectly good name. Very dignified." He swept the photograph and the silver medallion back into his bottom desk drawer and locked it.

Glory eyed the empty plastic tube that had just delivered her friends. "What the heck *is* that thing?"

A pleased look appeared on Sir Edmund's face. "I take it you haven't anything like it back in America?"

Glory shook her head. "Not at the Spy Mice Agency, at least."

"Our very own Tube," said the head of MICE-6 proudly. "Pneumatic tube, that is. Runs on forced air. The humans used them years ago to route messages through the building. The system has long been in disuse, but I had our lab fire it up a few months ago. Very efficient mode of internal transportation."

"Like a cross between a submarine and a roller coaster," whispered Squeak to Glory, climbing up onto the cork beside her.

"I think I'll stick to my skateboard," Glory whispered back. She smiled at her friends. Squeak Savoy was a sleek gray house mouse. She was cheeky and bright—she'd graduated at the top of her class in spy school—and she and Glory had instantly taken a liking to each other when they'd met in New York. Bubble Westminster was stockier, with brown fur, and he wore a bow tie like his boss. A church mouse (Cathedral Guild), he was characteristically quiet, but stouthearted and sharp as a tack.

"I have a job for the three of you," said Sir Edmund. "It's a local affair, something a bit out of our usual sphere of influence. But it involves one of Buckingham Palace's pet projects, and they've ordered all paws on deck for this one."

Buckingham Palace! Home of Britain's royal mouse family! Glory's elegant little ears perked up at this. This meant she was being asked to participate in—well, in a royal spy mission. She sat up a little straighter on her cork. *Here it comes,* she thought eagerly. *The start of my glamorous overseas career!*

"It seems the city's orphans have been disappearing at an alarming rate," explained Sir Edmund. "No one keeps accurate records of these street urchins, of course, and Scotland Yard is convinced they're simply being scooped up by stray cats." The elder mouse frowned. "In any event, the situation has come to the attention of the Prince of Tails and the Duchess of Cornmeal. As patron and patroness of the Nibbleswick Home for Little Wanderers, their royal highnesses have a keen interest in the safety of London's orphans. They've asked that all street mouselings be rounded up and either found proper homes or given permanent residence at Nibbleswick."

Sir Edmund nodded at the three spy mice seated before him. "I'd like you to help with the investigation. Bartholomew, you'll be out on the streets with the roundup team. Squeak and Glory, you'll be assisting with the interrogations. It's an assignment I feel calls for a feminine touch."

Glory and Squeak exchanged a dubious glance.

"These are orphans, after all. They may need a bit of mothering."

Squeak rolled her eyes at Glory. Sir Edmund was quite old-fashioned, and he had set ideas about the roles that females—in particular house mice like Squeak and Glory (who was half house mouse, thanks to her bakery-bred mother)—should play. Her boss saw Squeak's expression and frowned again. "I'll expect the three of you to fulfill your assignments with complete professionalism," the head of MICE-6 said sharply. "Best take the Tube up to the roof. Your pigeons are waiting—you're due at Scotland Yard within the hour."

Bye-bye, royal spy mission, thought Glory glumly. *Hello, dull police work.* There was nothing glamorous about rounding up street mouselings. Nothing at all. With a sigh, she nodded obediently and hopped off her cork. So did Bubble and Squeak.

Behind them, the door to Sir Edmund's office flew open with a bang. The head of MICE-6 whipped around. "Miss Honeyberry!" he cried in exasperation. "How many times have I told you—"

"Sir!" his secretary interrupted breathlessly. "You need to see this!" She scurried across the carpet and thrust a piece of paper into his paw. "Computer gymnasts just handed it in. It's from Intertail. Marked For Your Paws Only *and* urgent!"

"Thank you, Miss Honeyberry," said Sir Edmund, dismissing her.

Miss Honeyberry bustled out, and Glory gave Squeak and Bubble a worried glance. Intertail was the French equivalent of the Spy Mice Agency and MICE-6. Glory wondered what message could be so important that it needed to be marked both top secret and urgent.

"Oh, my," said Sir Edmund softly as he scanned the note. Something about his tone of voice sent a shiver down Glory's spine. Sir Edmund looked up. He regarded them somberly. "Brie de Sorbonne was just spotted outside a *boulangerie* in Paris."

47

The three agents looked at each other, aghast.

"But I thought—" said Glory.

"Didn't we—" said Bubble.

"Didn't they—" said Squeak.

Sir Edmund shook his head. "Apparently not," he replied. "According to this report, a Norwegian trawler dropped anchor in Oslo this morning. The *Dagmar Elisabeth*. She was carrying the *Mayflower* balloon in her hold. Her captain found it floating in the North Sea. Our computer gymnasts picked up the news on the Internet just as the message from Intertail came through."

The head of MICE-6 stared at them, his round black eyes deadly serious. "If Brie survived, chances are the others did as well," he said quietly. "You'll need to watch your tails. It appears that the rats are back."

CHAPTER 7

Stilton Piccadilly and
Roquefort Dupont peered up at
the office door in front of them.
Haltingly, the British rat read aloud
the name engraved on its brass
plaque. "D. G. Whiskers, Esquire." He nodded in satisfaction. "This is the place."

Dupont slanted him a suspicious glance. "So who is this 'Goldwhiskers' you've been yapping about all morning, anyway?"

"You'll see," Piccadilly replied smugly. He reached out and tapped on the bottom of the door with the tip of his tail.

"I still don't see why we need help," grumbled Dupont. "Especially not human help."

His companion smiled slyly. "Did I say he was human?"

Dupont's fierce red eyes widened in surprise.

Above them, an intercom on the wall crackled to life. "Place all deliveries on the floor to the right of the door, please," stated a polite female voice.

Stilton Piccadilly stretched up on his hind paws, placing his snout as close to the intercom speaker as he could reach. "No deliveries," he replied. "We're here to see Goldwhiskers."

"Goldwhiskers?" There was a long pause. "I'm afraid there's no one here by that name. Now if it's D. G. Whiskers, Esquire, whom you'd like to—"

"Cut the malarkey," snarled Piccadilly. "Tell him it's me, Stilton Piccadilly."

The intercom went silent. A moment later the rats heard a slight whirring noise overhead, and they looked up to see a security camera zooming in. It inspected them for a few moments. Then, near the floor to the right of them, a panel in the wall slid open.

Stilton Piccadilly stepped over an envelope on the carpet and swaggered through the opening. Roquefort Dupont followed more cautiously, dragging Fumble along on his leash. The panel slid shut behind them.

The two rats and their captive mouse looked around. The office they were standing in was empty. Not a human was in sight. No one sat at the ornate desk; no one sat on the plush sofa; no one stood by the big window overlooking the Thames.

"So where is this Goldwhiskers of yours?" whispered Dupont.

A trapdoor in the ceiling clattered open, and a basket appeared, tied to a rope. It descended slowly, settling onto the floor in front of them with a slight bump.

"Going up?" called a deep, melodious voice from somewhere beyond the trapdoor. "Third floor, housewares and fine china! Fifth floor, gentlemen's undergarments!" The voice gave a booming laugh.

"Ha very ha," sneered Piccadilly in reply, climbing into the basket. "You always were a joker."

Dupont sniffed the basket suspiciously. It smelled faintly of strawberry jam. His stomach rumbled. He'd only managed to scavenge a bit of bread and cheese at the airport before stowing away on the flight from Oslo, and that was hours ago. He was starving. A hungry Dupont was a mean Dupont, and he jerked angrily on the leash as he climbed in beside his British colleague. Fumble tumbled over the edge behind him, landing in a dejected heap.

"Heave away, mouselings!" ordered the deep, melodious voice. The basket swayed back up toward the trapdoor.

As it came to rest on the cubbyhole floor, Piccadilly hopped out and looked around. He gave a low whistle. "You must be doing well for yourself," he said. "Your digs are a bit fancier than last time I was here."

Dupont stared up at the enormous rat seated in the leather chair before them. The rat's whiskers glittered in the sunlight. "Oh I get it," he said sarcastically. "Gold*whiskers*. I guess that kind of thing passes for clever over here."

"Who is your rude friend?" Goldwhiskers asked Piccadilly.

"He's not my friend," Piccadilly replied. "But his name is Dupont."

"Ah, yes," said Goldwhiskers.

Dupont swelled importantly. "I take it you've heard of me," he gloated. "The name's Roquefort Dupont, actually. Great-great-great-great-great—"

Goldwhiskers flicked his paw, cutting him off. "Yes, yes, I know," he said with a yawn. "Related to Camembert Dupont, who used to live in a castle, et cetera, et cetera. Current headquarters in a sewer beneath Dupont Circle in Washington, D.C."

Dupont looked stunned. He wasn't used to being interrupted. He didn't like being interrupted. His eyes blazed an angry red.

Stilton Piccadilly gave him a warning kick. "We've known each other a long time, right, Double G?" he said, laughing nervously and inching closer to the leather chair.

"Aha!" said Goldwhiskers. "I thought as much. The only time my old sewer mates look me up is when they need something. Out with it, then. What is it you want?"

Piccadilly flushed. "Just to give you the chance to return a favor, that's all," he said. "You haven't forgotten all those times I saved your tail, have you? Back when you were just plain-old, ordinary Double Gloucester Whiskers?"

"That was a very long time ago," said Goldwhiskers silkily. "Another life. It can be dangerous, stirring up the past."

Piccadilly squirmed. "I need your help. A favor. For old times' sake."

Briefly, he outlined the events of the past month—the showdown with the mice and their human friends in New York, which had gone unexpectedly sour; the disastrous balloon crossing over the Atlantic—and how tomorrow night's

Christmas Eve gala at the Royal Opera House offered them a sudden, unexpected opportunity for revenge.

"Revenge?" said Goldwhiskers. He shook his head in disgust. "Will you sewer crawlers never learn? You're no better than cats—so busy chasing mice, you never look up long enough to see there's a better way to do business." He gestured at his lavish lair. "Look at all this! Do you really want to live underground forever, eating nothing but human garbage?"

Dupont nudged Piccadilly. "See? That's exactly what I've been trying to tell you! We could be living in a castle!"

Goldwhiskers snorted. "A castle? Oh, please. Have you ever actually visited a castle, Dupont? They're drafty and cold and full of mildew." He shivered dramatically, then gazed around his snug cubbyhole with satisfaction. "Give me a penthouse in the city any day of the week."

Piccadilly shook his head stubbornly. "Revenge is the rat way, Double G. Claws and jaws! Have you forgotten that?"

Goldwhiskers inspected his own manicured claws. "That is so twentieth century," he replied. "And so typical of you, old chap. You have no vision. If you want to get ahead, you need to get with the program. Upgrade. Set your sights higher. Otherwise, you'll be left in the dust. Even the mice are more advanced than you."

"What are you talking about, 'upgrade'?" Dupont burst out resentfully. "We can read!"

"About time," sneered Goldwhiskers.

Dupont lunged. Piccadilly jerked him back.

"Rats that want favors should show more respect,"

whispered Goldwhiskers, his cultured accent slipping a bit. His eyes glinted dangerously.

The phone on the table beside the red-leather chair interrupted them with a shrill ring. Twist, who had been watching the proceedings wide-eyed, leaped straight up into the air in alarm and came down on Farthing's tail. The tiny mouseling squealed and puddled on the carpet.

"Silence!" ordered Goldwhiskers. He glared at Farthing. "Someone clean up that mess! And get this creature out of my sight!"

As the still-squealing Farthing was hustled off toward the far corner of the cubbyhole, Dodge hopped onto the table. She leaped onto the speakerphone button and nodded at Goldwhiskers.

"D. G. Whiskers, Esquire," said the big rat.

A voice on the other end of the phone launched into a rapid-fire report. Dupont and Piccadilly strained to decipher the words, but they made no sense at all.

"Yes," said Goldwhiskers. "Yes, I see. Very wise, Fleming. You have my permission to sell." He nodded to Dodge, who leaped onto the button again in response, ending the call.

"My broker," Goldwhiskers explained to his guests with a wink. "Oil has peaked."

"You have a stockbroker? A *human* stockbroker?" asked Dupont.

"Of course. Don't you?" replied Goldwhiskers with a smug smile.

Roquefort Dupont stared at the big rat. He was beginning

to feel inferior. Dupont didn't like feeling inferior. He was accustomed to being the meanest, most powerful rodent everywhere he went. A tidal wave of rage surged through him. It was time to knock this big, arrogant rat off his leather chair and onto his big, arrogant tail. Dupont lunged forward.

Once again, Piccadilly jerked him back.

"I'll let you two chaps in on a little secret," said Goldwhiskers, leaning forward. His voice dropped to a whisper. "You know what makes the world go round? It's not revenge. It's not claws and jaws. It's *money*."

Stilton Piccadilly and Roquefort Dupont eyed him suspiciously.

Goldwhiskers nodded. "That's right, chaps. Our ancestors did live in castles, and you can live in castles again—if you're dead set on it. Or in penthouses or villas, or aboard yachts. Anywhere you please. But you're not going to get there by feuding with the short-tails. That misses the entire point. One thing and one thing only is going to land you in the lap of luxury, and that's cold, hard cash."

"And where exactly do you get this cold, hard cash?" scoffed Piccadilly.

A crafty look settled over Goldwhiskers's snout. "I have my ways." There was a knock at the door of the office below. "That will be lunch," he said. "Silence again, everyone! Dodge?" He motioned to his valet, who leaped onto another button on the table beside him, this one for the intercom. "May I help you?" she said politely into the speaker.

"Delivery for D. G. Whiskers, Esquire," came the reply.

"Place it on the floor to the right of the door, please," instructed Dodge. "You'll find an envelope there waiting for you."

"Right. Ta, luv."

Goldwhiskers flicked his tail toward a screen that hung on the wall opposite from them. "Take a look at this," he said. "My latest toy. Cost me a pretty penny."

Dupont and Piccadilly watched as Dodge leaped onto yet another button, activating the surveillance camera. An image flashed onscreen: the office door and the hallway beyond. A human delivery boy placed a large box on the floor, collected the payment envelope that had been placed there for him, and walked briskly away.

Goldwhiskers grinned at his visitors. "See? This is what money can do for a rat with vision. Everything I could possibly want, delivered right to my doorstep."

"Don't they get suspicious?" asked Dupont, fascinated in spite of himself.

"The humans?" Goldwhiskers shook his head. "Suspicious of a businessman who's a bit of a recluse? Who's a bit eccentric? Come now, surely even an ignorant Yank like yourself must know that London is full of eccentrics. What's one more? Especially one who tips as well as I do."

The mangy hackles on the back of Dupont's thick neck bristled angrily at the insult, but before he could reply, Goldwhiskers cracked his tail. "Fetch, mouselings!" he ordered, and the orphans sprang into action. A dozen or so leaped into the empty basket; the rest lined up along the rope and lowered it through the trapdoor to the office below.

"Watch and learn, chaps—watch and learn," said Goldwhiskers to his visitors proudly. "You can't lead the high life without an entourage." He eyed Fumble pointedly, then smirked at Dupont. "And one pathetic mouse doesn't count."

Goldwhiskers turned back to his mouselings. "That's right," he said soothingly. "Your obedience makes Master so happy. And you mouselings like to make Master happy, don't you? When Master is happy, everyone is happy. Master gives food. Master gives warmth. Master gives all good things."

"We thank you kindly, Master, giver of all that is good," chanted the mice in automatic reponse.

As Roquefort Dupont listened, he pictured himself seated in a big red-leather chair back in his lair at Dupont Circle. He pictured himself with mice to do his bidding and humans at his beck and call. A smile creased his hideous snout. He liked what he saw.

"Money can do this, you say?" he demanded. "Cold, hard cash?"

Goldwhiskers nodded, and Dupont chewed on his thin rat lip thoughtfully.

"Where would mouselings be without Master?" Goldwhiskers continued. "On the street! No one wants useless orphans. No one but Master. And what happens to *lazy, disobedient mouselings*?" The big rat's voice rose sharply, and the orphans quailed. "That's right! The *oubliette*!"

"The oobly-what?" whispered Dupont.

Piccadilly shrugged. "Not a clue."

"'Oubliette,'" Fumble replied listlessly from behind them. "It comes from French. It means 'forgotten place.' He's talking about a dungeon."

"Which reminds me," added Goldwhiskers. "Where's Farthing? An extra slice of cheese for whoever brings me my naughty pet!"

The mice who weren't pulling on the dumbwaiter's rope scattered in search of the youngest orphan. A tiny squeak of alarm was heard in the shadows as someone nabbed him, and Farthing was duly dragged back to the red-leather chair.

Goldwhiskers glared down at him. "Haven't I warned you about my carpet?"

Farthing popped his tail into his mouth and sucked on it anxiously.

"Don't you want to stay here, close to Master, where Master can feed you and take care of you and keep you safe?"

Farthing nodded, his bright little eyes wide with fear.

"Then why do you keep PUDDLING ON MY CARPET?" roared Goldwhiskers. "Master has no choice but to put you back in the oubliette until you learn some manners!"

"I need an oubliette," said Dupont enviously as the tiny orphan was seized and dragged away. He yanked on Fumble's leash, and the mouse toppled nose first onto the floor. "Remind me to build one when I get back to Washington."

"Yes, boss," said Fumble tonelessly.

Behind them, the basket swayed up through the trapdoor,

piled with packages and mice. Goldwhiskers rubbed his paws together with greedy glee. "Smoked salmon, crackers, an assortment of cheeses, and for the main course, wild-mushroom pie. Oh, and for dessert, fresh raspberries and whipped cream."

Roquefort Dupont's stomach growled loudly.

"Fresh raspberries? In December?" Piccadilly was incredulous.

"I ordered them online this morning. You can get any-thing at Fortnum and Mason's," Goldwhiskers explained. "All it takes is money."

"Quite the racket you've got going here," said Dupont with grudging admiration.

"One does one's best," Goldwhiskers replied modestly.

"So, will you help us, Double G?" asked Piccadilly.

Goldwhiskers frowned. "What's in it for me, chaps? I assume you haven't any cash to offer."

Piccadilly scratched a filthy ear, considering. "How about membership in the G.R.R.?"

"Your silly little club?" Goldwhiskers laughed scornfully, and Dupont's hackles rose again. "I have no interest in petty rodent politics. Let's take a look and see what else you might have to offer me." He clapped his paws. Dodge sprang to atten-tion. "Laptop, please," ordered the big rat. Dodge gave a sharp whistle, and the mouselings crowded around a rolling table, angling it in front of the red-leather chair.

Dupont and Piccadilly watched in astonished silence as Goldwhiskers reached out his tail and tapped rapidly on the keyboard. Dupont felt another swelling of inferiority, followed quickly by envy, then fury.

"Let's see what Mr. Google has to say about our visitors," said Goldwhiskers, talking softly to himself as he typed. "Ah, here we are. Christmas Eve gala at the Royal Opera House, followed by an exclusive reception. That much we know already. Wait, here's a news update from Reuters. Looks like they arrived at Heathrow safe and sound and checked into the Savoy. How convenient—they're right next door."

"Just give us a time and a place, and we'll take it from there," said Stilton Piccadilly.

Goldwhiskers eyed him. "You will, will you? Trust me, you'll need much more than just a time and a place." He inspected the computer screen again. "Hmmm. Grand tour of London planned today for the accompanying family—now, that could be interesting." Something else caught his eye, and the big rat straightened up in his chair. "What's this? Dinner and dancing tonight at the Tower of London? Now that is *definitely* interesting." He gave his two guests a sly glance. "Perhaps we might work together after all."

"What time is all this stuff—the tour and that dinner?" said Dupont, a trifle belligerently. It was bad enough being on unfamiliar turf and having to hand over the reins to Stilton Piccadilly. Now Goldwhiskers was starting to take control. Roquefort Dupont's tail began to thrash back and forth.

Goldwhiskers ignored him. He tapped on the keyboard again. "We'll need their itinerary. Just need to hack into . . . the Savoy's . . . records. Right, here we go." He clapped his paws together again. "Twist! Where's Twist?"

The throng of mice parted as Twist stepped forward. Goldwhiskers leaned down from his thronelike chair and placed a large paw on the mouseling's thin shoulder.

"Time to test your mettle," he said. "The Savoy, room 607. Make it snappy. You're looking for a piece of paper with a tour schedule on it."

The mouseling nodded and started to go.

"Oh, and Twist?"

Twist paused, looking back at the big rat expectantly.

"Keep an eye out for sparklies," said Goldwhiskers. "No use letting a good opportunity go to waste. The mother is a diva. She knows she's meeting royalty. She'll have brought along her best."

Twist nodded obediently and melted into the shadows.

"Sparklies?" said Roquefort Dupont. "What the heck are sparklies?"

"All in good time, my American friend," Goldwhiskers replied. "All in good time." He nodded at Dodge, who leaped onto the back of his chair and tied a crisp white linen napkin around his thick gray neck. "First things first. Smoked salmon, anyone?"

CHAPTER 8

DAY ONE
DECEMBER 23
1015 HOURS

"But I don't want to see the Changing of the Guard!" whined Priscilla Winterbottom. Their limousine was parked in front of the Royal Opera House. The two sopranos were standing beside it. "I've been to Buckingham Palace a million times before!"

Prudence Winterbottom poked her head back into the vehicle. "Now Priss," she chided, "remember what I told you. You are the hostess today, and good hostesses wear cheery faces in public! Buckingham Palace is a high treat for our American guests."

Priscilla shot a resentful look at her American guests.

"Please?" coaxed her mother. She thrust a wad of cash into Priscilla's hand. "Here," she said. "Buy yourself something nice at Harrods afterwards. The driver is going to drop you all there for lunch. Won't that be fun? A little shopping? Ice cream and treats at the Chocolate Bar? A ride on the Egyptian Escalator?"

Priscilla was not to be jollied out of her ill temper. She flounced in her seat, giving Nigel Henshaw a spiteful jab with her elbow as she did so.

"Ouch!" cried Nigel, recoiling.

"Don't be such a baby," snapped Priscilla. "It was an accident."

She glared at her mother. Her mother glared back. *Ferret senior and ferret junior squaring off for a fight,* thought Oz. He nurtured this little fantasy for a moment, imagining a limousine full of flashing fangs as the mother-daughter duo scrapped and tussled in the backseat.

Lavinia Levinson tugged on her colleague's arm. "Come along, Prudence," she said. "They're expecting us in rehearsal. Luigi will sort it all out."

With a defeated sigh, the British soprano withdrew. Ignoring Priscilla, who was still glowering, Oz's mother leaned in, gave Oz and his father each a kiss on the cheek, and smiled at D. B. and Nigel. "Have fun, kids!"

As the limousine drove off, Priscilla Winterbottom glared at Nigel Henshaw, who hugged his arms around himself and stared at the floor. Oz and D. B. gawked at the city through the windows.

No wonder James Bond chose to live here, thought Oz as they passed Trafalgar Square and St. James's Park. London was beautiful. Maybe he'd live here too when he was a grown-up spy. Lost in this pleasant daydream, he nearly jumped out of his seat when Priscilla kicked him in the shin.

"This is all your fault!" she snarled. "If it wasn't for you and your stupid mother, I wouldn't be here."

Oz stared at her, casting about frantically for a comeback and coming up empty-handed as usual. D. B. was much better at this sort of thing. He usually thought of snappy things to say about three days later, when it was far too late to matter. "Leave my mother out of it," he mumbled finally, prodding at his glasses. *Pathetic*, he thought, even as the words left his mouth. Oz wished desperately that James Bond were here. Agent 007 would know exactly how to deal with Priscilla Winterbottom.

Priscilla's junior ferret lips stretched out in a sneer. Her junior ferret eyes narrowed. Beside her, Nigel Henshaw scooted as far away as he could. He'd obviously seen that look before, Oz realized. So had he, unfortunately. It was a shark look. Cold. Calculating. Searching for weak spots. Sadly, he had many to choose from.

"You want to know something else about your mother?" Priscilla said, softly so that the adults in the front seat wouldn't overhear. "She's fatter than mine, and her voice is nowhere near as good. I heard Mr. Henshaw say so. Didn't he, Nigel?"

Nigel looked around desperately for rescue, but Oz's father and the limousine driver were still deep in conversation. Priscilla Winterbottom reached out and grabbed the boy's scrawny arm. She gave it a sharp twist. He winced and cried out. "I said, 'Didn't he, Nigel?'"

Nigel's pale blue eyes flicked quickly toward Oz in

wordless appeal. He nodded unhappily, and Priscilla released him.

D. B. leaned forward. "You know, if I had a name like Priscilla Winter*bottom,* I'd be keeping my stupid mouth closed," she warned.

Priscilla flushed an angry red. She glared at D. B., then threw a calculating glance toward the front seat. Poking her lower lip out, she squinched up her eyes and wailed suddenly, "Mr. Levinson! They're making fun of my name!"

Oz's father turned around in his seat. Priscilla took a hankie out of her pocket and wiped at her eyes dramatically. "Wa-aa-aah!" she wailed again, louder this time, peeking over the edge of fabric to see if her phony tears were having the desired effect.

They were. Luigi Levinson frowned. "Oz, D. B., I'm ashamed of you," he scolded. "Picking on poor Priscilla! When you've only just met. You know better, the both of you. What would your mother think, Oz?"

"But—" Oz started to protest.

"He didn't—I didn't—" stammered D. B.

Oz's father shook his head. "I don't want to hear another word from either of you," he said. "Not until you apologize to Priscilla."

He stared at them somberly from beneath his shaggy black eyebrows. Oz's face flushed. He glanced over at D. B., who was squirming in her seat at the injustice. Behind her hankie, Priscilla smirked.

"I'm waiting," said Luigi Levinson, drumming his fingers impatiently on the seat back.

"Sorry, Priscilla," mumbled Oz finally.

"Me too," muttered D. B.

"There, that's better," said Oz's father. "You children behave yourselves now." And with that, he turned back to the limousine driver.

A smug smile played across Priscilla Winterbottom's lips. Oz and D. B. exchanged a wary glance. Priscilla gave new meaning to the term "shark." Most of the sharks they knew avoided getting grown-ups involved like the plague. But they were in altogether different waters with Priscilla. They'd have to navigate their way very carefully.

Priscilla's foot shot out, and she kicked Oz in the shin again. He flinched. "My mother is definitely a better singer than yours," she whispered, baiting him.

Oz shrugged, defeated. If he said anything at all, she'd just tell his father another lie and get him into more trouble.

"Why don't we let the audience be the judge of that at the concert tomorrow night?" suggested D. B.

Priscilla eyed her suspiciously. "Fine," she said finally. "You might be in for a surprise, though. Right, Nigel?" Her hand shot out and she pinched the younger boy on the leg. Hard. Nigel whimpered and nodded.

The limousine came to a halt in front of Buckingham Palace. The back door opened, and Luigi Levinson reached in with a bearlike arm and plucked Priscilla from her seat. "Feeling better, my little sugarplum?" he asked. She nodded tremulously. Dabbing at the corner of one eye with her hankie, then turned and smiled triumphantly over her shoulder at Oz and D. B.

"Good. Come along, then, all of you," said Oz's father, herding Nigel out as well. "They'll be starting the ceremony soon, and we want to get a good spot up in the front."

Oz and D. B. followed, exchanging an uneasy glance.

"She's awful," said D. B.

"Horrible," agreed Oz. "Worse than Jordan and Tank."

"And she's up to something," added D. B.

"I know," said Oz unhappily. The question was, what? Oz sighed. He hoped Glory's vacation was off to a better start than his.

CHAPTER 9

DAY ONE
DECEMBER 23
1115 HOURS

Glory's vacation was not off to a better start, unfortunately.

"Come on then, lad, out with it," said Inspector Applewood, the sturdy brown field mouse from Scotland Yard with whom she had been paired.

The grubby mouseling seated across the table from them gave his runny nose a furtive swipe. "I told you already—I don't know nuffing, guv," he whined.

Glory sighed. It had been like this all morning. Not an orphan in London knew a thing about the disappearances. Inspector Applewood hadn't even been able to get them to tell him their names. Glory had tried too, but it was clear that the detective resented her presence, and she had quickly given up. Scotland Yard had not been at all happy to have agents from MICE-6 foisted upon their investigation.

Inspector Applewood closed his notebook. "Right then, lad, you can go," he told the street urchin. He turned to

Glory. "See?" he said. "Told you. It's cats, plain and simple. We don't need an investigation. And we don't need any help from MICE-Six. You might as well leave now too."

Glory was sorely tempted to do so. She glanced out the window as a Pigeon Air taxi swooped by. On its back she spotted a pair of tourist mice. They snapped pictures of Scotland Yard and then flew on. That's what she should be doing right now too—touring London, not interviewing stubborn mouselings.

"Wait," she said, as the orphan hopped off his perch and started to leave. Glory reached into her backpack and pulled out the remains of breakfast. She pushed the napkin-wrapped object toward the mouseling, who sniffed it hopefully.

"That is hardly necessary, Miss Goldenleaf!" protested Inspector Applewood. "He'll be fed when he arrives at Nibbleswick, just like the others."

Glory ignored him. "It's all yours if you cooperate," she told the orphan. "You know, help us out."

A crafty look settled on the youngster's sharp little face. "If I talks, I gets it all to meself?"

"All to yourself," Glory promised.

The mouseling wiped his nose with his paw again, considering. Then he shrugged and climbed back up onto the cork perch. Inspector Applewood frowned. The mouseling started to reach for the crumpet. Glory whisked it away. "Oh, no," she said, "fair's fair. You first. What's your name?"

The mouseling's bright little eyes were fixed firmly on the crumpet. His stomach rumbled loudly. "Smudge," he said.

"Smudge what?" asked Glory.

The orphan shrugged. "Dunno. Just Smudge."

Glory tore off a corner of the crumpet and passed it to him. "Well then, Smudge, I'm sure you know that orphans just like you have been disappearing?"

The mouseling nodded, his cheeks bulging with crumpet.

"I'll bet that's a bit scary, isn't it?" said Glory sympathetically. She tore off another corner of the crumpet and passed it across the table. The mouseling wolfed it down hungrily. "Your friends disappearing like that, I mean."

Tears welled up in the orphan's bright little eyes. He pawed them angrily. "I'm not scared of nuffing," he boasted.

Glory passed him another piece of crumpet. "No, I can see how brave you are. Brave as my brother B-Nut, almost, and he's a pilot."

Smudge's mouth dropped open. "A pilot? Wicked! I wants to be a pilot someday."

"I'm sure you shall," said Glory. "A bright young mouse like you can go far in life. So back to these friends of yours. Do you have any idea where they're off to? Maybe Inspector Applewood is right—maybe it's just cats?"

The mouseling cast a sidelong glance at the detective. For a minute, the only sound in the room was the chewing of crumpet. "Not cats," he said finally.

"What makes you say that?" Glory replied.

Smudge leaned across the table toward her. "No bones," he whispered. "Cats leave bones. When me mates disappeared, there wasn't nuffing. Not even a whisker."

Glory turned to Inspector Applewood. "He's got a point," she said. The detective frowned and scribbled furiously in his notebook.

"So if it's not cats, what do you think it is?" In a bold gamble, Glory thrust the remainder of the crumpet across the table toward Smudge and held her breath. It was all or nothing now. The mouseling tore into the crumpet greedily. He glanced around fearfully while he ate, as if perhaps someone might be watching, or listening. Finally, he leaned toward Glory again and whispered, "They calls him Master."

"Who calls him Master?" she whispered back.

"The ones he takes," replied Smudge.

Glory regarded him thoughtfully. "Did you get that, Inspector Applewood? They call him Master."

The detective glared at her but dutifully recorded the information in his notebook. Glory turned back to the mouseling. "And who is this 'Master'?"

Smudge shrugged. "Dunno," he said. "Only been one what was taken that ever came back. That were last summer. She wouldn't say nuffing at all. At night sometimes, though, she had dreams. 'Master,' she'd say. 'Please, Master, not the oobly . . .' The oobly-something! No one knew what she was on about."

The room grew quiet as Glory and the Scotland Yard detective digested this information. *So London has a boogeymouse,* thought Glory. *A boogeymouse named Master who is kidnapping orphans.* The question was, why?

CHAPTER 10

DAY ONE
DECEMBER 23
1630 HOURS

"Where are we?" whispered
Roquefort Dupont.

He poked his mangy snout out of
the drainpipe he'd just crawled
through and looked around cautiously.
There were humans nearby. He could hear them. And it was
always best not to attract attention when there were humans
nearby.

Stilton Piccadilly shouldered past him. His fierce red
eyes widened in surprise as he, too, looked around. "The
Tower of London?" he said. "Double G, why did you drag
us out here?"

Goldwhiskers smiled and hopped down out of the
drainpipe onto the ground below. "You'll see," he replied,
his whiskers glittering in the last rays of late afternoon sun.

Dupont hopped down beside the big rat. He yanked on
the leash in his grimy paw, and Fumble tumbled to the
ground as well. Behind him sprang Dodge and Twist, followed by Stilton Piccadilly. Goldwhiskers held up a paw in

warning and pointed toward a stone bridge far above them. On it stood a human. He was dressed from head to toe in a scarlet uniform.

"It was here, through this very gate, that the boatmen would pass with their cargo of doomed prisoners!" he boomed.

The rats froze as the tour guide pointed directly at the heavy, arched wooden gate beside them.

"Nobody move a muscle," whispered Goldwhiskers.

A crowd of tourists leaned over the stone wall and stared at the gate. They didn't seem to notice the small cluster of rodents at its base.

"Imagine for yourselves that final voyage of terror!" continued their guide. "Down the Thames and under London Bridge, where sharp pikes displayed the heads of the unfortunate who had passed through the gate before you. Would that be *your* fate?" He swooped his large hand down atop the head of a boy in the audience, who squealed obligingly in response. "Imagine the torches, their flames throwing eerie shadows upon the dank stone walls! Imagine the cries from the prisoners being tortured! Imagine the horror of it all!"

The guide shivered. So did his rapt audience.

"Sounds like my kind of party," whispered Dupont.

"Shush!" ordered Goldwhiskers.

"You shush!" retorted Dupont. Stilton Piccadilly gave him a warning poke. He grumbled, but he fell quiet again.

"Through this very gate they'd pass," continued the

human above them. "Queens, dukes, earls, and princes, many of them never to be seen or heard from again. Do you know what they called this gate? They called it"—he paused for dramatic effect, raising his arm again—"Traitors' Gate!" The man brought his arm down in a chopping motion, like an axe, and the crowd shrieked and cheered.

The tourists moved off. "Follow me," Goldwhiskers said, leading the way. Fumble, who was still attached to his ragged leash, pulled up the rear, staggering beneath the weight of a duffel bag bulging with gear.

The rodents disappeared behind a loose stone in the base of the Tower's thick wall, reemerging a few seconds later on the other side. They scuttled across the gravel walkway to the Bloody Tower—"where two young princes vanished into eternity," the guide, several yards farther down the gravel path, informed his audience—and squeezed through a crack in the ancient building's foundation. They reappeared momentarily in the inner courtyard; then, clinging to the shadows that skirted Tower Green, they darted past the ancient execution block toward a building on the far side of the walled fortress's interior.

"Any idea where he's taking us?" Dupont whispered to Piccadilly.

Stilton Piccadilly shook his head. "Haven't been here in years. Played about in the dungeons and grounds as a ratling—terribly exciting, as I recall. Especially when the ravens would chase us. They keep ravens here, you know. Always have."

Goldwhiskers stopped at the base of yet another enormous stone building. WATERLOO BARRACKS was posted on a sign outside.

"What does all this have to do with our plan for revenge?" demanded Dupont." You'll see," said Goldwhiskers again. "This way."

He squeezed into a downspout and scrabbled up it onto the roof. The others followed, trailing after the big rat as he squeezed into a ventilation duct that led into the barracks' thick stone walls. Plunged into darkness, the rats and mice gripped each other's tails in a long rodent chain as Goldwhiskers nosed his way back down, down, down into the building. "Two lefts, a right, another left, and—this is it! Here we are!" His voice rose with excitement as they finally emerged into a narrow space behind a heavy mesh screen.

Only a dim light filtered through the screen's heavy grid from the room beyond. Roquefort Dupont sniffed at the metalwork suspiciously. It was solid and imposing, impenetrable to humans, but the holes in the grid were not impossible for a small rodent to slip through. Even he might be able to manage it, what with all the weight he'd lost at sea.

Dupont peered out into the room on the other side. Thick, whitewashed stone walls muffled the noise of the tourists, who were standing on what looked like a moving sidewalk. They were being whisked past something. Dupont wasn't sure what; the crowd of humans was blocking his view. The room had two entrances, one at either end. Both were shielded by enormous steel doors reinforced with enormous steel hinges and locks.

"Whatever the humans have locked up in here must be pretty valuable," he observed to Piccadilly in a low voice.

"You have no idea," Piccadilly replied. "I just figured out where we are."

"Where's that?"

"The Jewel House."

"Jewel House?" Roquefort Dupont twitched his ugly snout. "Never heard of it."

"As in the Crown Jewels? You know, those things the royal humans wear when they're being royal."

Understanding dawned on Dupont slowly. "So that's what Goldwhiskers meant by sparklies!" His beady red eyes narrowed. He turned on the big rat, his thick tail whipping back and forth angrily. "You double-crossed us! You said you were going to help us, but you're just helping yourself!"

"Don't fret, my American friend," said Goldwhiskers, a note of amusement in his voice. "Trust me, there'll be plenty to go around by the time we're done."

"I'm not your friend," snarled Dupont. "And I have no interest in your ridiculous sparklies, or whatever you call them."

Goldwhiskers shrugged. "Then you're a bigger fool than I thought." He fiddled with something he had taken out of the duffel bag on Fumble's back and placed on the floor.

Curiosity got the better of Dupont. He grunted and nudged the object with his snout. "What's that?"

"My BlackBerry," Goldwhiskers replied. "A small hand-held computer, really."

"Let me guess. Cold, hard cash, right?"

Goldwhiskers grinned. "You're catching on, Dupont. A rat's got to pay, if a rat wants to play." He watched as Dodge deftly connected the device to a wire that ran along the top of the heavy gridded screen. "We'll be overriding a few systems here."

"You sound like a mouse," sneered Dupont. "They're always fiddling with human gadgets."

"Exactly," said Goldwhiskers. "That's what keeps them two steps ahead of you, Dupont—haven't you figured that out yet?"

Dupont's tail thrashed angrily again. Piccadilly placed a warning paw on his shoulder. "Don't touch me," snarled Dupont, shrugging it off. "Don't ever touch me."

"Aha, here we go," said Goldwhiskers, ignoring them both.

Curiosity won out over anger again, and Dupont and Piccadilly drew closer. A schematic of the building's electrical and computer systems flashed onto the BlackBerry's screen. It looked like a pile of spaghetti.

"What's that?" sneered Dupont. "The menu for an Italian restaurant?" He snickered at his lame joke.

Goldwhiskers pointed at the screen with his tail. "We'll need to shut it down here and here," he told Dodge, who nodded and scampered away. Then he looked over at Twist. "Do you know what you need to do, mouseling?"

"Yes, Master," Twist replied obediently

Goldwhiskers nodded in satisfaction. "Then you will please Master, and you will feast tonight!" he promised. "More food than you can possibly imagine, if you and Dodge do your jobs right."

"How about us?" demanded Dupont. "What do we do?"

Goldwhiskers turned back to his two rat companions. "What do we do?" he replied. "Simple. We wait."

CHAPTER 11

DAY ONE
DECEMBER 23
2030 HOURS

"THEY'RE GONE!" shrieked
Lavinia Levinson.

A diva's shriek can shatter glass,
and it quickly brought Oz, his father,
and D. B. running.

"What's gone, darling?" asked Luigi Levinson anxiously.

"My rubies!" wailed Oz's mother.

"Are you sure?" said her husband.

Lavinia Levinson nodded. She held her jewelry case
upside down over her bed and shook it. Nothing came out.
"I was going to wear the earrings tonight, the ones the
Italian ambassador gave me after I sang at La Scala. They're
so festive, and they match my outfit."

She looked sadly down at her flowing, floor-length caf-
tan. It was made of red satin and covered in red spangles.
Oz thought it made his mother look even more like Mrs.
Santa Claus than her red wool cape.

"The ruby earrings? The bracelet and necklace, too?"

"Gone! All gone!" wailed Oz's mother.

Oz's father rushed to the phone and called hotel security. In short order their lavish suite was bustling with concerned staff.

"This is dreadful!" said the hotel manager. "Simply dreadful! I can assure you that we at the Savoy will do everything in our power to see that your jewelry is returned to you, Mrs. Levinson. I only wish you'd entrusted it to our hotel safe."

Oz's mother dabbed at her eyes with a hankie and nodded. "I was planning to, but then I had to rush to rehearsal almost the minute we got here, and I simply forgot."

Scotland Yard arrived in full force, and Oz heard the hotel manager whisper the words "cat burglar" to the detectives. One of them approached Lavinia Levinson. "So sorry we have to meet under these circumstances, madam. I'm a devoted fan."

"Thank you," whispered Oz's mother, dabbing at her eyes again. "You're too kind."

The detective whipped out a notebook and pen. "Would you like to tell me what happened?"

Sniffling, Lavinia Levinson nodded. "Well, I was getting ready for a party—we were all getting ready for a party—"

The detective looked up. "The one at the Tower of London? I read about that in the papers."

Oz's mother nodded again. "Yes, that's the one. Anyway, I went to put on my ruby earrings, and they weren't there. I thought maybe I'd put them in a drawer, or tucked them inside a shoe—good hiding place, you know, shoes—but no. And then I checked and all my other jewelry was gone as well!"

"Would you mind if we inspect the room while you're away—for fingerprints and such?" asked the detective.

"That would be fine, Inspector," replied Oz's father. "I do hope you'll find the thief who did this."

"We'll do our very best."

It was a subdued ride to the Tower of London. Oz's parents held hands silently in the back of the limousine. Oz and D. B. stared out at the passing city. London was lit up for the holidays, and they passed shop after shop whose windows glowed with gaily decorated Christmas trees and brightly wrapped packages. High above the streets, strung between the tall lampposts, were strands of twinkling snowflakes. The glitter did little to lift their spirits, however.

Oz leaned over to D. B. "I tried to get in touch with Glory," he whispered, pulling his CD player from his pants pocket. Thanks to Bunsen's tinkering, it was now a radio transmitter and receiver preset to the Spy Mice Agency's frequencies. "She didn't answer."

"She's on vacation, Oz, remember?" D. B. whispered back.

Oz shrugged. "I know, but I still thought it might be worth a try. Maybe she can help somehow."

"A mouse catching a cat burglar?" D. B. snorted. "I don't think even Glory's up to that."

The limousine slowed as it approached the Tower, bumping its way over the broad cobblestone drive toward the front gate. A security guard checked their invitation, then waved them through.

"It's showtime," said Oz's father, as they pulled up in front of an imposing stone building. He climbed out and extended a hand to his wife. "No more long faces, now!"

"You're right, dear," said Oz's mother, managing a weak smile. "It's only jewelry, after all."

Her husband gallantly kissed her hand. "Which you, Lavinia, with your natural sparkle, don't need to look beautiful."

Oz's mother's smile broadened. "Thank you, dear. You look very handsome too. Just like James Bond."

"A tuxedo makes any man look like James Bond," said Oz's father, winking at Oz. "Even a shaggy bear like me."

Oz's mother leaned down and kissed her son on the cheek as he emerged from the limo. "You look just like James Bond Junior, sweetie."

Oz reddened and plucked awkwardly at his bow tie. For the first time in his life, he actually felt a bit like James Bond. Except for his shoes. He gazed down at them glumly. Finally, his chance to wear a tuxedo, and he'd blown it. He'd forgotten his black dress shoes. They were still at home in his closet. He was stuck wearing the brown museum grandpa shoes instead. Luckily, with all the excitement, his parents hadn't noticed.

"And you look equally smashing," said Lavinia Levinson, patting D. B.'s cheek. "That yellow dress makes you look like a princess."

"I can't believe I'm finally going to see the Crown Jewels!" D. B. crowed, bouncing excitedly up and down. She thrust her program at Oz. "See, Oz? After dinner, there's dancing and a private viewing of the jewels just for us. It's gonna be awesome! No crowds, no long lines."

Oz, who had been shown the program repeatedly over the past few hours, nodded absently.

A limousine pulled up beside them, and Prudence Winterbottom climbed out. The British soprano was dressed in a silver gown, and she was practically encrusted with diamonds. Diamond earrings, a diamond necklace, diamond bracelets, diamond rings—even a diamond tiara. "Lavinia, darling!" she cooed. "You look lovely!" Her sharp ferret eyes bulged in surprise as they traveled from Oz's mother's bare ears to her bare neck and arms. "No jewels tonight?" she said. "Saving them for the concert tomorrow and the royal reception, are you?"

Oz's mother pressed her lips together.

"Stolen," said Oz's father.

The British soprano gasped. "No! What happened?"

"Scotland Yard is on the case," Luigi Levinson continued. "Apparently there's a jewel thief on the loose."

"The cat burglar!" exclaimed Prudence Winterbottom. "I've been reading about him in the papers." She adjusted the tiara in her poof of ferret curls and slanted a glance at her jewelry-less American colleague. "Pity," she said smugly.

Oz frowned. Clearly, Prudence Winterbottom didn't think it was a pity at all.

There was a barrage of blinding flashes as a horde of reporters spotted the divas and began snapping photos.

"Is it true the two of you are rivals?" demanded one, thrusting a microphone under the two women's noses. "Can we look forward to a Christmas Eve battle of the sopranos?"

"Rivals? Battle?" Prudence Winterbottom laughed a fake tinkling laugh. "Whatever gave you that impression! Lavinia and I are the dearest of friends."

"That's right," said Oz's mother, with a bit more sincerity. "We're here to sing together. It's Christmas, after all."

Oz and D. B. were squeezed to the edge of the crowd as the reporters surged forward to follow the two opera stars inside.

"Do all Americans wear such strange shoes with tuxedos?"

Oz whirled around. Priscilla Winterbottom was standing behind him, along with Nigel Henshaw. She smiled, and her sharp little ferret teeth gleamed in the distant flash from a camera. *Amazing,* thought Oz. Even Jordan and Tank on their best days didn't have the kind of shark skills that Priscilla Winterbottom had. She'd managed to zero right in on his Achilles' heel in two seconds flat. *Make that Achilles' shoe,* he thought morosely, gazing down at his toes.

"Put a sock in it, Prissy Slushbutt," said D. B. "Nobody cares about Oz's shoes."

Priscilla gaped at D. B. Her cheeks flamed bright red. She opened her mouth to reply, then snapped it shut again. Grabbing the hapless Nigel Henshaw by his reedlike arm, she stuck her nose in the air and flounced off after her mother, dragging the conductor's son with her.

"*Prissy Slushbutt!*" crowed Oz, slapping D. B. a high five. "I wish I'd thought of that!"

D. B. looked pleased. "Winterbottom—Slushbutt. It's a natural," she explained. "I've been waiting to spring it on her ever since this morning."

Oz gazed at his friend in admiration. D. B. was so much quicker on her feet than he was when it came to dealing with sharks. He made a mental note to himself for future reference: *Anti-Shark Tactics 101: A swift counterattack can be highly successful in repelling the foe.*

Dinner dragged on in a blur of toasts and speeches accompanied by more courses and silverware than Oz had ever seen in his life. ("Why do we need seven forks?" he whispered to D. B. at one point.) Priscilla Winterbottom, who was seated next to Nigel across the wide table, made a point of ignoring them, except to glare occasionally over her roast beef and Yorkshire pudding. After the remains of dessert (a spectacular Christmas trifle) were cleared away, the hired orchestra swung into a medley of up-tempo holiday tunes.

Over at the head table, Mr. Henshaw stood up and extended his hand to Oz's mother. Luigi Levinson quickly stood up and did the same to Prudence Winterbottom. Around the room, chairs emptied as couples headed for the dance floor.

"Come along, Nigel," ordered Priscilla Winterbottom, pushing back her chair.

Nigel wilted in his seat. Priscilla grabbed his ear and twisted it. "I said, come along!"

The younger boy had no choice but to obey. As Priscilla dragged him onto the dance floor, D. B. leaned over to Oz. "That poor kid might as well have 'shark bait' tattooed across his forehead," she said.

Oz nodded in agreement.

D. B. threw down her napkin. "Oh well, nothing we can do about it now," she said. "Time to go see the jewels."

Oz trotted after his classmate. Outside the banquet hall, a guard in a scarlet uniform—"He's called a Yeoman Warder, or Beefeater," D. B. informed Oz—directed them across the courtyard to the Waterloo Barracks. They passed through the building's heavy wooden doors, followed by the increasingly faint strains of "Rudolph the Red-Nosed Reindeer."

"It's kind of creepy in here, isn't it?" said D. B., shivering slightly. The building's stone walls and stone floor were as chilly as the night air.

"No kidding," said Oz. "Where is everyone? You wouldn't think we'd be the only ones who'd want to see the jewels, would you?"

D. B. shrugged. "I guess everyone else would rather dance."

The two children followed the signs to the exhibit, pausing to watch a short video that explained some of the history behind the collection.

"There they are!" squealed D. B., as they entered the Jewel House. She raced over to the moving walkway. It whisked her toward the glass display case. Oz followed, nodding to the lone security guard who watched them from his post by the door. A heavy steel door, Oz noted. Nearly as thick as the stone walls.

Oz's eyes widened as the walkway carried him closer to the glass cases. D. B. was right; these weren't just any old jewels. There were swords and scepters, crowns and corona-tion finery, and gems the size of goose eggs. All of the glit-tering regalia was spread out before them in a breathtaking display. Even his mom's rubies paled in comparison. So did Prudence Winterbottom's diamonds.

"Look!" cried D. B. "The Koh-i-Noor."

"The Koh-i-what?" asked Oz, as they were carried slowly past an impressive crown trimmed in purple velvet and white ermine.

D. B. pointed to the huge gem that adorned the front of it. "The Koh-i-Noor diamond," she said. "It means 'moun-tain of light.' It was given to Queen Victoria in 1850. It's more than a hundred carats."

The walkway deposited them at the end of the display near the exit door. "Let's go through again," urged D. B., herding her friend back along the raised platform beside it.

"Maybe we're not supposed to," said Oz, glancing ner-vously at the guard.

"It's okay—nobody else is here."

Again and again the two allowed themselves to be car-ried past the display of jewels, as D. B. explained to Oz what he was looking at. "That's the Sovereign's Orb," she said, pointing to a golden ball with a diamond-encrusted cross atop it. "And the Imperial State Crown. It's got a ruby on it that's one of the biggest in the world. And that's the Sovereign's Ring." It was the Koh-i-Noor, though, that drew her like a magnet. "It's on the Queen Mother's crown," she said. "Did you know it's supposed to be cursed?"

"The Queen Mother's crown?" said Oz in surprise.

"No, you goof, the Koh-i-Noor," replied D. B. "It brings misfortune or death to any male who wears it. Females are safe, though. That's why it was made into a crown for a queen."

"Do you really think that's true?" Oz said, staring at the big diamond.

D. B. shrugged. "Who knows?"

"Can we go now? The guard's gonna think we're casing the joint," said Oz finally, after following D. B. past the display a dozen times.

"This place? Come on, Oz, it's like Fort Knox," said D. B. She glanced over at the guard, who was pointedly checking his watch. "Maybe you're right. It is nearly midnight. Your parents are probably wondering where we went. Once more and then we'll go, okay?"

The guard crossed his arms on his chest and scowled at them as they ran back for yet another pass.

"We're almost done!" called D. B. "Promise!"

"What do you think something like that would be worth?" asked Oz, peering closely at the Koh-i-Noor diamond as they approached it again.

"Millions, I guess," said D. B. "Maybe billions. I don't know."

As the moving walkway conveyed them for the final time toward the Queen Mother's crown, the lights overhead flickered. The walkway gave a small electronic whine. The guard looked over at them and frowned. The lights flickered again, and the walkway slowly ground to a halt.

"Oi!" cried the guard. "Wot you kids up to over there?"

"Nothing," D. B. called back.

The lights flickered a third time and went out. The room was plunged into complete darkness.

Oz had never experienced such darkness. The blackness that swallowed them was absolute. Not a pinpoint of light shone anywhere. The room's thick stone walls blocked everything out. It was like being in a cave.

"Oi!" cried the guard again. "Stay where you are!"

Oz and D. B. heard the sound of his footsteps, and a grunt as he grappled with something on the wall. The guard's walkie-talkie crackled to life. "Clive?" said a voice. "Everything under control down there?"

They heard the guard scrabble for his receiver. "Power went out," he reported. "Trying to locate the auxiliary."

Oz flinched as something brushed past his ankle. "What was that?" he cried.

"What was what?" cried D. B., clutching his arm.

Something brushed past Oz's other ankle. He shrieked. So did D. B.

"Oi, you lot!" cried the guard. "I said don't move!"

There was a loud *click*—the guard throwing a switch, perhaps—but nothing happened. Another crackle from his walkie-talkie. "Any luck?"

"Auxiliary's not working either," the guard reported.

"I'll bring a torch," the voice on the walkie-talkie replied. "How many you got in there with you?"

"Just a couple of kids."

"Right. Be along in a minute, then." The walkie-talkie crackled again, then went silent.

"Where'd you kids go?" demanded the guard.

"Right here!" D. B. replied. "We haven't moved an inch!"

Oz heard a tiny *clink* beside him. Or at least he thought he did. The hair on the back of his neck stood up. "What was that?" he cried again.

"What was what?" cried D. B., clutching his arm again.

"Did you hear that?"

"WHAT?"

"Will you kids shut up! There's no need to panic!" shouted the guard, beginning to sound panicked.

"Do you think this place is haunted?" Oz whispered anxiously. "Maybe it's the curse of the Koh-i-Noor."

"Oz, stop! You're scaring me!"

They heard the heavy tread of footsteps as the guard approached. "Wot you two nattering about then?" he asked.

"Nothing," said Oz. A hand clamped down on his shoulder. He jumped.

"There you are!" the guard said in triumph. Relief, too—

Oz could hear it in his voice. The guard was as nervous as he was. *Maybe this place really is haunted,* Oz thought, as goose bumps crept up his arms.

"Ouch," said D. B. "That's my hair."

"Sorry," said the guard. "You two stay right here by me. We'll be safe together. They're coming to fetch us any minute."

The seconds ticked by. Standing in the pitch black, the only sound that of their own breathing, Oz tried not to think about the cursed diamond that lay just two feet away. Or the prisoners who had languished and expired here in the Tower. Or the dungeons or the torture chamber or—

"Where are you?" called a deep voice, and Oz jumped again. A flashlight's beam pierced the darkness.

"Over here!" replied the guard named Clive. "On the walkway!"

Light bounced off his glasses, and Oz blinked. "You kids all right?" asked the deep voice.

Oz and D. B. nodded.

"How about you, Clive? Weren't scared, were you?" The other guard snickered, and Clive suddenly let go of Oz.

"Nah," he replied, crossing the room to join his colleague.

Oz saw the flashlight's beam flicker along the wall, then settle on a large red switch. The guard with the deep voice threw it, but as before, nothing happened. "Ned, fire up the emergency auxiliary in sector seven, would you?" he said into his walkie-talkie.

A few seconds later, the walkway whined back into life. It jerked forward, throwing Oz against D. B. The two of them toppled over in a heap.

"Oof," said D. B.

"Sorry," said Oz.

Overhead, the lights flickered once, twice, then held. Oz and D. B. stood up and brushed themselves off.

"You kids best be going," called Clive. "Party's almost over."

"Okay," Oz replied.

"Better do a quick security check first," said the other guard, and began circling the room. "Everything looks fine to me."

"Me too," said Clive. He stepped onto the walkway and moved toward the jewels. "Nothing broken, nothing out of place." He froze. "Oi," he said weakly.

"What?" said the other guard. Clive pointed wordlessly at the display case.

D. B. gasped, and this time Oz was the one to clutch her arm.

The Koh-i-Noor had vanished.

CHAPTER 12

The display reads:

DAY TWO
DECEMBER 24
06:00 HOURS

"En garde!"

Two mice—one white, one gray—circled each other warily. Each held a fencing foil (made from the tip of a broken knitting needle) at the ready in his paw. Each wore a fencing mask (cleverly fashioned from bits of mesh from an old screen door) that obscured his face.

Clack-clack! Clack-clack! Clack-clack-clack-CLACK! The knitting-needle foils darted this way and that as the two thrust and parried, slashing at each other fiercely.

"I have you now!" crowed the white mouse, forcing his opponent into a corner.

"Not so fast," puffed the other.

As the white mouse moved to press his advantage, the gray mouse ducked and twirled, leaping nimbly out of reach. The white mouse whirled around, but it was too late. He froze as his opponent's foil made one final thrust, stopping just a whisker's width away from his throat.

Both mice stood motionless for a moment; then the gray mouse removed his mask. "Well done, Mr. Burner!" said Julius Folger, head of Washington D.C.'s Spy Mice Agency. "I'm seeing much improvement in your skills." He patted his stomach, panting slightly. "And these dawn workouts aren't doing my waistline any harm either."

Bunsen Burner, lab-mouse-turned-secret-agent, removed his mask as well. "Thought I had you at last," he said ruefully.

"One of these days you will, if you keep practicing," Julius replied. "Same time tomorrow, then?"

Bunsen nodded in agreement. As they turned to go, the door to the fencing room flew open. A computer gymnast rushed in, clutching a scrap of paper in her paw.

"Sorry to interrupt, sirs!" she squeaked. "But this message just came in. It's marked most urgent."

Julius scanned it, frowning.

"It was encoded," the computer gymnast added. "Took us a few minutes to decipher. It's from Glory Goldenleaf."

Bunsen's pale ears pricked up. A message from Glory? Marked urgent? Was she in trouble? His nose turned an anxious shade of pink.

"We managed to decipher everything but this last bit," the gymnast continued, tapping the bottom of the page with her paw. "We can't figure out what those x's and o's are supposed to mean."

The tip of Bunsen's nose deepened to scarlet. He knew exactly what those x's and o's were: kisses and hugs. A secret message for him from his sweetheart.

Julius Folger cleared his throat. "I see," he said, glancing over at Bunsen. "Well, don't give it another thought, Miss Eiderdown. Thank you for your help." He turned to Bunsen as the small house mouse bustled out of the room. "Absence makes the paws grow fonder—eh, Mr. Burner?"

"Sorry, sir," mumbled Bunsen. Technically, agents weren't supposed to include personal messages in official communiqués.

"Well, I suppose I'm not such a fossil that I can't recall those days myself," said Julius. "I remember one time, years ago, when Mrs. Folger and I—" He broke off and harrumphed again. "But enough of that foolishness." He looked down at the piece of paper in his paw. "I'm afraid this isn't good news at all."

Bunsen peered over his boss's shoulder. "'Crown Jewels stolen,'" he read aloud. "'Oz and D. B. under interrogation at Scotland Yard.'" His pink eyes widened. "Oh, my," he said. "Does Glory mean Scotland Yard thinks that Oz and D. B.—"

"It would appear so," said Julius.

"But this is serious!"

"Very," agreed Julius.

"The poor children!" cried Bunsen, wringing his pale paws. "They must be frightened out of their wits. And here we are an ocean away, and not a thing we can do to help them!"

"Steady, Mr. Burner, steady," said Julius. "There's plenty we can do to help them. I'm going to contact Sir Edmund, first of all, and find out what MICE-Six knows. As for you—well, in addition to being a promising field agent and splendid fencing partner, just remember that you are the brightest and best lab mouse this agency has ever had."

Bunsen blinked at this unexpected praise.

"How's that prototype of yours coming along?" Julius continued. "A.M.I., I mean?"

"Well, she's not completely up and running yet, but initial tests have been positive," the lab mouse replied cautiously.

"Splendid," said the elder mouse. "The carpets are being cleaned on the fourth floor before the museum opens this morning, and the administrative offices will be crawling with humans any moment. I've recalled the night shift computer gymnasts downstairs as a precaution. Perfect time to take our new gal for a spin."

He led the way to the lab through the warren of hallways and offices that made up Spy Mice Agency headquarters. It was early still—Pigeon Air flights wouldn't begin bringing commuters to work for another hour or two—and the lab was deserted.

Bunsen scampered over to a cupboard on the far side of the room. He reached into a pocket of his utility belt and produced a small key, then unlocked the cupboard door.

"Here she is," he said nervously, whisking away a white handkerchief to reveal what looked like some sort of bizarre sculpture. "Artificial Mouse Intelligence. A.M.I. for short."

Julius inspected the contraption. A.M.I. was the first-ever

mouse-built computer, a goal the agency had been working toward for quite some time now. Currently, they had to rely on human computers, which the gymnasts could only use after hours at the museum to lessen the risk of being spotted by museum employees. Being spotted was forbidden; it could mean a visit from the exterminator. Besides rats, there was nothing that any mouse feared more than a visit from the exterminator.

Foraging the right parts for A.M.I. had been slow—a microchip here, a microprocessor there—but just this past week Glory's brother Chip had scored a small, collapsible keyboard (tossed into a garbage can outside a dormitory at Georgetown University), and Bunsen himself had finally solved the monitor problem. This had been their biggest hurdle. Even the smallest laptop monitor, had they been able to forage one, would be too tall to fit in the agency's headquarters beneath the floorboards of the Spy City Café. Bunsen had been the one to suggest hot-wiring A.M.I.'s hard drive to a handheld game player and using its screen. His idea had worked beautifully—at least in initial tests.

Julius put in a call to the typing pool, and in two shakes of a cat's tail Miss Eiderdown reported back for duty.

"You have Paws Only clearance?" Julius asked. The computer gymnast nodded.

"And you've had practice on A.M.I.?" Bunsen added.

The computer gymnast warily eyed the laboratory ceiling—to which a thick layer of quilt scraps had been stapled—and nodded again, reluctantly this time.

"Good," said Bunsen, handing her a safety helmet. Similar to the one he used on his skateboard, it was fashioned from a bottle cap. Inside, however, it contained an extra-thick layer of foraged sponge. Miss Eiderdown fastened it securely and gave him a nod.

"A message to Sir Edmund Hazelnut-Cadbury, MICE-Six, London," Julius began, clasping his paws behind his back and pacing back and forth. "Just heard the news, stop. Agents in peril, top priority their release, stop. Our full resources at your disposal, stop. Please advise, stop."

As he rattled off his message, the computer gymnast sprang onto the small keyboard, flipping and tumbling and diving from one letter to the next. She squeaked twice—first when she banged her head against the ceiling while leaping for the *C* in "Cadbury," and the second time when she did it again while performing a triple somersault onto the *p* in the final "stop." Working on A.M.I. was hazardous duty, for unlike the human offices upstairs in the museum, the agency's own offices had low ceilings. There had been one concussion already this week, along with several slightly dazed gymnasts.

"Well done, Miss Eiderdown," said Julius after she finished.

His employee smiled wanly, rubbing her head. "Anything else?"

"Google, please," said Bunsen, and Miss Eiderdown again leaped and twirled. "Scotland Yard."

Once on the home page for Scotland Yard, Bunsen

issued a series of crisp orders, keeping a close eye on the screen. Miss Eiderdown obediently tapped in various strings of code, hacking into the website. It didn't take Bunsen long to find the file about the missing jewels—and the two human suspects.

His pink eyes narrowed as he scanned the report on the screen. Beside him, Julius read along, stroking his tail thoughtfully.

"'Koh-i-Noor diamond and Sovereign's Ring missing,'" Bunsen read aloud. "'Well-planned theft of detachable gem and small, portable ring most likely carried out by two American children.'" He shook his head glumly. "Look here," he continued, tapping the screen. "They found the secret compartment in Oz's shoe. They think he planned to hide the Koh-i-Noor in it."

"And they found his CD player as well," added Julius. "That must be how Oz got word to Glory."

Bunsen tugged unhappily on his ears. "This is terrible!" he moaned.

"Keep reading," said Julius. "It gets worse. They think Oz's parents are accomplices. Listen to this: 'Suspect's mother reported theft of her own jewelry from the Savoy earlier in the day, likely as decoy. Mentioned shoe as a good hiding place. Possible nervous slip?'"

The head of the Spy Mice Agency and the lab mouse regarded each other soberly.

"This is not good," said Bunsen. "Not good at all."

CHAPTER 13

DAY TWO
DECEMBER 24
1130 HOURS

"What are we supposed to do with THIS?" roared Roquefort Dupont, hurling the ring that Goldwhiskers had just given him across the floor. It bounced to a stop in the far corner of the cubbyhole, where Farthing, who had been released from the oubliette, was cowering. The tiny mouseling squeaked in alarm and darted away as fast as his little legs would carry him, taking shelter behind Twist. "It's a *ring,* not *revenge!*"

"Are all Americans this dim, or is it just you?" said Goldwhiskers. He was typing away on his laptop keyboard, the Koh-i-Noor beside him, safely wedged into the seat of his red-leather chair. Every few seconds he paused to admire it. "Aha, here we are." He swiveled the laptop around toward Dupont and Piccadilly, and pointed wordlessly at the screen.

"What?" demanded Dupont.

Goldwhiskers sighed. "I thought you said you could read."

The hackles on Dupont's thick neck rose angrily. "I can!"

"Well then, what are you waiting for?"

Dupont shot him a murderous glance and scowled at the screen. "After last night's shocking Crown Jewels theft, Ozymandias Levinson and Delilah Bean, two American schoolchildren, were interrogated before dawn at Scotland Yard," he muttered aloud. He looked up at Goldwhiskers, who smiled.

"Wire service," the big rat said smugly. "Latest news flash. It'll be the main headline on every paper in the world in a few hours. Revenge enough for you?"

Dupont shrugged and nodded reluctantly.

"How about you, Stilton, old chap?"

"Don't forget the mother," Piccadilly replied.

Goldwhiskers smiled again. "Oh, don't worry—I haven't forgotten her. Twist!"

The mouseling scampered forward, Farthing clinging to his tail like a limpet. "Sir?"

"Where's that piece of paper you brought me yesterday, the one from the Savoy?"

Twist trotted off, returning momentarily with Lavinia Levinson's London itinerary.

"That's the one," said Goldwhiskers, plucking it out of his paw. He chortled with glee. "Oh, this is more fun than I've had in ages! Perhaps revenge does do a rat good now and then." He waved the itinerary at Dupont and Piccadilly. "It's bound to have her fingerprints on it, right? We'll just print the ransom note on the back, send it to

Scotland Yard, and bingo! One less soprano bellowing onstage."

He tapped out a few sentences on his laptop, then handed the piece of paper to Dodge. "Take this downstairs to the printer, would you?" he said. His assistant nodded and headed for the office below.

While they waited for Dodge to return with the ransom note, Farthing ran off in search of the ring. He retrieved it from the far corner where Dupont had thrown it and dragged it back to the red-leather chair. Squatting down on the carpet beside it, he patted it with his tiny paws. "Pretty!" the wee mouse cried, tracing the circle of diamonds that surrounded the ring's huge sapphire, and the rubies that crisscrossed its surface.

"More than pretty, my pet—priceless," said Goldwhiskers.

"It's a stupid human ring," grumbled Dupont.

"It's the Sovereign's Ring, you idiot—worn by the rulers of England," Goldwhiskers retorted. "It will fetch an enormous sum." He leaned forward in his chair. "That's cold, hard cash, remember? Which you and Piccadilly may share between you for your services. Enough to set you up in that castle you've been mooning about. Or perhaps your own island in the Caribbean? The two of you would make marvelous pirates."

A flicker of greed ignited in Dupont's red eyes. He glanced from the Sovereign's Ring to the Koh-i-Noor. "If the ring's so valuable, how about that? What's our share of the diamond?"

Goldwhiskers hesitated. He picked up the Koh-i-Noor in his manicured paws and gazed into its depths. "Ah, yes," he said. "Actually, there's been a slight change of plan."

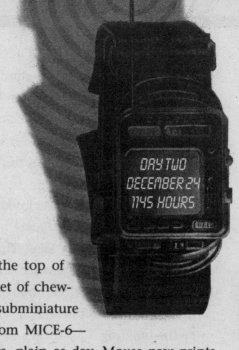

CHAPTER 14

DAY TWO
DECEMBER 24
1145 HOURS

Click! Click! Click!

Glory peeked over the top of what looked like a packet of chewing gum—in reality a subminiature spy camera, on loan from MICE-6— and frowned. Paw prints, plain as day. Mouse paw prints. No—mouseling paw prints, to be exact. A twin trail of them, creeping along the edge of the wall inside the Jewel House at the Tower of London.

"Check it out," she called softly. Bubble and Squeak scampered over as she pointed to her discovery.

"Fresh?" asked Squeak.

Bubble inspected the prints closely. "Looks like it," he reported.

"Let see where they go, then," said Glory, and clinging carefully to the shadows at the base of the wall, she started to follow the trail. Bubble and Squeak crept along behind her.

So much for my vacation in London, thought Glory

ruefully. Her Christmas break had quickly turned into a working holiday. Not that she minded—Oz and D. B. were infinitely more important than touring the city. Glory halted. In front of her, the paw prints suddenly veered off toward the center of the room—and the glass case.

"This is as far as we go," cautioned Bubble. "Mustn't risk being seen."

The exhibit—which was closed to the public pending a full investigation into the jewel heist—was crawling with detectives from Scotland Yard. The three spy mice agents had taken quite a risk getting even this far. Fortunately, their Pigeon Air flights had managed to avoid the security cameras on the roof, but they'd had a couple of close calls inside the building.

"But we've got to see where the trail leads!" Glory protested. "Two of our agents are at stake!"

"It was probably just a pair of little thrill-seekers, come to see what all the excitement's about," said Squeak.

"Maybe you're right," replied Glory. "But I still need to know for sure. Something smells fishy to me."

"How are we going to get from here," said Bubble, tapping the wall, "to there?" He pointed at the display case. "Without being seen, I mean."

Three pairs of bright little eyes scanned the room. Above them, bolted to the ceiling at regular intervals, were security cameras just waiting to catch their every move. Across from them stood a throng of sharp-eyed human investigators. It was hopeless.

Just then, there was a rumble in the hallway outside, and a guard pushed a cart into the room.

"Teatime!" he called out cheerfully, and the humans quickly crowded around.

"One down," said Bubble softly. "Bit of luck, that. But there are still the cameras."

"Wait a minute—I have an idea," said Squeak. She rummaged in her backpack and pulled out a large hankie. "A bit low-tech, but sometimes the simplest way is best. I found it in the lobby of the Savoy on the way to work this morning." She rubbed at a lipstick smudge in one corner of the fabric and frowned. "Just needs a bit of a wash and it'll be good as new. I'm going to give it to my mum for Christmas. She's been wanting a new bedspread for ages."

"So what's your plan?" asked Glory, puzzled.

In reply, Squeak draped the hankie on the floor. "Look—it's the same color."

"Squeak, you're a genius!" said Glory.

"I heartily agree," added Bubble. "The perfect camouflage! We'll be practically invisible!"

Each mouse grasped a corner of the hankie, and together they gave it a shake. As the square of fabric ballooned up, they quickly huddled beneath it. It drifted down, concealing them from view. Squeak poked her head out from under one side and glanced over at the humans. "Ready, steady—go!" she called, pulling her head back in. The hankie scuttled across the floor toward the glass display case.

Not a single Scotland Yard detective noticed. Not a single security camera whirred to life. The hankie bumped up against the display case and came to a halt. Three small furry heads appeared as the mice cautiously emerged.

"There!" said Glory triumphantly. She pointed to a crack at the base of the display case. It was small enough not to arouse the suspicion of human investigators, but large enough for a mouse to pass through.

"Do you really think a pair of mouselings could have pulled this off?" said Squeak.

Click! Click! Click! Glory's camera whirred. "I have no idea," she replied. "But if there's an opening above, and any sign of paw prints, we've got our man. Er, mouse, I mean. Mice. Whatever—let's go!"

Leading the way, Glory disappeared through the crack. Bubble and Squeak were right on her tail. A minute later, three little noses poked out beneath the Imperial State Crown.

"Oh, my," said Glory, dazzled.

Before them, stretching the length of the long display case, gleamed a bright river of gold and gems. The Crown Jewels of England! The trio of secret agents crept forward and craned their little necks up at the crown that had shielded them from view. Worn by human queens and kings at their coronations, it was enormous. Its surface glittered with diamonds, sapphires, pearls, and other precious stones. Affixed to its front, at center, was a glowing red stone the size of a pigeon's egg.

"The Black Prince's Ruby," whispered Squeak.

"Oh, my," said Glory again, her camera clicking furiously. "We don't have anything like this back in Washington." She contemplated the enormous ruby. "So why didn't that get stolen too? It must be worth a fortune."

"The Koh-i-Noor is the only stone in the collection that's detachable," explained Bubble. "Whoever pulled this off knew exactly what they were doing."

Squeak nudged them. "Look!" she said softly. "A paw print."

Sure enough, impressed very faintly into the velvet that draped across the display case in front of them was a single, tiny paw print.

Click! Click! Click! went Glory's camera. "I still don't get it," she said, looking up at her colleagues. "It doesn't add up. What mouselings do you know that could mastermind a stunt like this? Even if they did manage to grab the Koh-i-Noor and the ring—then what?"

"The answer's got to be here someplace," Squeak replied. "Let's go back down and see if we can pick up the trail again."

The three spy mice withdrew beneath the Imperial Crown and reemerged a minute later at the base of the display case.

"Hurry," urged Bubble, casting an anxious glance over at the knot of humans by the cart. "Teatime's nearly over."

Once again using the hankie as a shield, the mice quickly retraced their steps to the shadows of the far wall. They fanned out and began searching for more paw prints. Several minutes ticked by. Then—

"Here!" cried Squeak excitedly. "Look, these ones lead in a different direction!"

Glory and Bubble rushed over.

"Looks like the two of them were dragging something heavy," said Bubble, pointing to a wide swath in the dust between the twin trails.

"Like a diamond and a ring?" suggested Glory, her camera clicking furiously as she photographed the crime scene.

"Hard to say," Bubble replied. "But look here—the trail just stops."

The mice frowned at the floor. He was right.

"A cat got them, perhaps?" suggested Squeak.

Bubble shook his head. "No cats allowed in the Tower," he said. "On account of the ravens."

"It's a dead end," said Squeak, disappointed.

"Not necessarily," Glory replied. She pointed to the ventilation grate in the wall above them. "Did either of you happen to bring along your grappling equipment?"

In reply, Bubble reached into his backpack and pulled out a fishhook. Tied to it was a long piece of dental floss. Swinging it expertly around his head, he flung the fishhook up at the grating. It wound itself around the metal grid and caught. Bubble tugged on the line to be sure it was secure, then passed it politely to Glory. "After you."

"Thanks," she said. Grabbing the floss in her front paws, Glory braced her hind paws against the wall and hauled herself swiftly up. Squeak followed, and Bubble brought up the rear, keeping a sharp eye on the humans.

"They must have gone through here," said Glory, clinging to the grating and peering into the darkness beyond.

"Pretty slick for a pair of mouselings," said Squeak.

"Not if our boogeymouse was directing them," Glory replied. "I'm beginning to think these two cases are related."

Bubble nodded in agreement. "I think perhaps you're right," he said.

"But what mouse would do such a thing?" cried Squeak. "Steal from humans, I mean?"

"Don't forget our old friend Fumble," said Glory. "It wouldn't be the first time a mouse did something dishonorable." She pulled up the line of dental floss and dropped it through the grating to the darkness below. "We need evidence, though, if we're going to help Oz and D.B."

Bubble and Squeak stared at her, horrified. "You mean we'd tell the humans at Scotland Yard that a mouse did this?"

Glory patted her camera. "We wouldn't exactly have to break the Mouse Code and *talk* to them," she explained. "We could just return the jewels, along with a few photographs. Humans are pretty smart; they'd put two and two together."

"They'd never believe it," said Bubble. "Not in a million years."

"We have to try," said Glory. "This is Oz and D. B. we're talking about. They're true-blue—and they're innocent. A criminal is a criminal, no matter how many legs he or she has. We need to find the Koh-i-Noor and the Sovereign's Ring and bring these misguided mice to justice. Here."

Glory reached into her backpack and pulled out a trio

of small headbands (cloth-covered elastic hair bands dropped by girls who visited the Spy Museum). Glued to the middle of each was a tiny lightbulb foraged from a discarded penlight. Glory gave one to each of her British friends, then strapped her own to her forehead. "Bunsen sent these along," she said. "Another new invention. He got the idea from some human TV show about cave explorers. Thought they might come in handy."

"I've always wanted to go spelunking," said Bubble happily. He switched on his headlamp, and a tiny beam shot out into the darkness. Squeak and Glory switched theirs on as well, and the three mice rappelled down into the dusty gloom.

"Nothing much back here," said Squeak, her voice echoing in the empty crawl space.

The trio of slender beams crisscrossed this way and that as the mice looked around.

"Wait!" called Squeak in excitement. "Look over there! More paw prints!"

Flash! Flash! Flash! Bubble and Squeak blinked as Glory photographed the twin trails of prints. "The two of them were definitely dragging something," she reported. "There's that same mark again."

Bubble leaned down closer to the floor, squinting at a flurry of paw prints. "What happened here?" he asked. "Looks like a scuffle of some kind."

"An ambush, do you think?" asked Squeak.

Once again, the slender beams from the mice's headlamps crisscrossed back and forth in the gloom. But aside from the trail of paw prints and the scuffle marks in the dust, there was nothing else to be seen.

"Whatever happened, they obviously escaped through there" said Bubble. He pointed to the far end of the crawl space. "The paw prints dead-end in front of that duct."

"We'd better report back to HQ," said Squeak. "And we'll need to talk to that mouseling again—what was his name?"

"Smudge," said Glory.

"Right. He'll be at Nibbleswick by now."

"One of us should rendezvous with Oz and D. B. They still need to be debriefed," said Bubble.

Glory's camera clicked rapidly as she took a few final photographs. "It's so frustrating," she said to her British friends as the three of them started to clamber back up the line of dental floss. "I feel like we're so close to an answer." She shook her head.

As she did so, the beam from her headlamp brushed the far edge of the crawl space, just beneath the ventilation duct. Out of the corner of her eye, Glory caught a glint of something. She paused, squinting in the gloom.

"Hang on a sec," she said, and slid back down to the floor. She scurried over to investigate.

Glory stooped down and plucked something off the floor. She held it up to the light. It was a whisker. A gold whisker.

CHAPTER 15

DAY TWO
DECEMBER 24
1145 HOURS

"What do you mean there's been a change of plan?" demanded Roquefort Dupont, his beady eyes narrowing in suspicion.

"Exactly what I said," replied Goldwhiskers. He stroked the Koh-i-Noor lovingly. "I'm going to keep it. I've waited all my life to own this diamond."

"You double-crossing, conniving, GREEDY SACK OF RAT GUTS!" Dupont advanced toward the red-leather chair, his tail whipping back and forth menacingly.

Goldwhiskers fanned the air in front of his snout with an enormous paw. "Has anyone ever told you that you have halitosis?" he said in disgust.

"Quit trying to change the subject," snarled Dupont, then hesitated. "Hali-what-sis?"

"Bad breath. It's rather off-putting. Dodge!" Goldwhiskers looked around for his assistant. "Breath mint!"

Dodge retrieved a mini-tin from the box on the table,

pried it open, plucked out a round white mint, and passed it to her employer.

Roquefort Dupont's red eyes blazed in anger. "Why, you no good, uppity—" He lunged toward Goldwhiskers. The big rat waited calmly until the last second, then leaned forward and popped the breath mint into the American rat's ugly, snarling snout.

"Agghh!" cried Dupont, toppling backward. He lay on the plush carpet, eyes watering. He coughed and gagged. "That tastes terrible!"

"Curiously strong, isn't it?" agreed Goldwhiskers. "Don't worry, you'll live. And your breath will smell much better too. Now, you were saying?"

"What—do—you—mean—you're—going—to—keep—the—Koh-i-Noor?" Dupont managed to choke out, still flat on his back on the carpet.

"I've changed my mind about ransoming it," Goldwhiskers replied coolly.

"I wouldn't be too thrilled to have that in my possession," said a mild voice.

The rats glanced over to where Fumble was seated on the floor.

"What business is it of yours?" demanded Goldwhiskers, clasping the Koh-i-Noor to himself protectively.

"It's supposed to be cursed," said Fumble, plucking idly at his frayed leash.

"Rubbish," snapped Goldwhiskers. "Everyone knows that's just an old rats' tale."

Fumble shrugged. "If you say so."

Goldwhiskers glared at Dupont. "Shut that ridiculous pet of yours up," he ordered, eyeing Fumble with distaste.

"He's not my pet; he's my slave," said Dupont, still coughing.

"Whatever."

Stilton Piccadilly swaggered up to the red-leather chair. "Dupont's right, Double G," he growled. "You double-crossed us!"

"Did I?" said Goldwhiskers. "I don't recall promising that I'd ransom the diamond. And I certainly didn't sign a contract. I would remember that. As my lawyer says, one should always get things in writing." He leaned forward in his chair. "What I *did* promise you was revenge. The humans are now in the custody of Scotland Yard, aren't they? Shamed, humiliated, soon to be carted off to prison? Isn't that enough?

Dupont staggered upright onto his paws. He gave a mighty swallow, shuddered as the breath mint went down, then shouldered his way over beside Piccadilly.

"What about cold, hard cash?" he demanded. "You promised us that, too."

Goldwhiskers pointed at the Sovereign's Ring. "There's more money right there in that ring than you could possibly dream of," he replied. "Enough for castles, villas, Caribbean islands—all of it and more. And if that's not enough for you, if it's more revenge you're after—claws and jaws and all that nonsense—there are a great many other things money can buy."

"Like what?" sneered Dupont.

"Like wreaking a little havoc amongst the short-tails as well as the humans," replied Goldwhiskers. "Money could buy you exterminators, for starters."

Piccadilly and Dupont exchanged a glance.

"Lots and lots of exterminators," said Goldwhiskers encouragingly. "What do you say, boys? Would you like to spread a little Christmas cheer, rat-style?"

Dupont's red eyes narrowed again as he considered the possibility.

"Now you're talking," said Stilton Piccadilly, growing excited. "Can you imagine the G.R.R.'s reaction, Dupont? We'd be voted into power for life."

"We?" growled Dupont. "There is no 'we.' I'm the Big Cheese, remember?"

Piccadilly glared at him. "You promised me second-in-command!"

"Did you get it in writing?" Dupont taunted. "Like your friend here says, I don't remember signing a contract."

"Why, you double-crossing—"

"Chaps, chaps," said Goldwhiskers in a soothing tone. "Don't let's get distracted. You can sort out the politics later. Is it exterminators you want? You get death and destruction; I get to keep the Koh-i-Noor?"

Reluctantly, the two rats turned away from each other and shrugged.

"It's a deal!" cried Goldwhiskers. "Dodge! Credit card!"

His efficient assistant rummaged through the lacquered box on top of the table and pulled out the rectangle of plastic—gold, naturally. She slapped it into her employer's waiting paw.

"Now then," murmured Goldwhiskers, turning to his laptop once again. "We'll want Rodent Rooter, of course. They're the biggest outfit in London. Plus, I like their jingle. 'Call Rodent Rooter . . .'" He hummed the tune from the extermination agency's commercial as he typed. "Looks like we're too late for anything this evening. They need eight hours' notice for bookings and cancellations. We'll have to settle for Christmas morning instead. Perfect! How jolly." He looked up. "Shall we schedule simultaneous attacks? They tend to be the most terrifying."

Piccadilly and Dupont nodded.

"Right, then," said Goldwhiskers briskly. "How do a thousand trucks sound?"

His two rat companions nodded again, even more vigorously this time.

"One thousand trucks—one thousand exterminators. Done," said Goldwhiskers, adding, "I'll have to offer a bonus, of course, since it's Christmas. Triple overtime holiday pay should do it."

As Goldwhiskers finalized the arrangements on his computer, the head of London's rat forces began to pace back and forth with excitement.

"Think of it, Dupont!" Piccadilly gloated. "From Mayfair to Marylebone, Southwark to Soho—we'll strike at every corner of the city! Kensington! Chelsea! Marble Arch and Notting Hill!"

"On Christmas Day, every mouse's favorite holiday!" added Dupont, his eyes glowing like hot coals as he pictured the devastation.

"Tomorrow, London—after that, the world!" Piccadilly cried, and the two rats slapped each other a high paw.

"That's more like it, chaps," said Goldwhiskers. "Nothing like a little holiday spirit." He smiled. "I think we'll call it Operation S.M.A.S.H.: 'Stop Mice and Stop Humans.' The mice get exterminated—you're happy. The humans get blamed for the robbery—I'm happy. I get to keep the Koh-i-Noor—I'm happy again. Oh, yes," he said. "I can see it's going to be a happy Christmas all around this year."

"For the rats, anyway," said Dupont, and he bared his fangs in an evil grin.

CHAPTER 16

DAY TWO
DECEMBER 24
1530 HOURS

The lab at MICE-6 was bustling with activity. Along one counter (a rectangular building block covered with tinfoil) a pair of white lab mice analyzed the golden whisker. One of them peered at it through a magnifying glass (foraged from the lens of a broken microscope) and offered comments to the other, who dutifully recorded them in a tiny notebook. Glory's photographs were pinned to a scrap of corkboard above the counter. A cluster of field agents examined them, frowning and scribbling notes.

The door to the lab swung open, and Sir Edmund Hazelnut-Cadbury strode in. Glory was right behind him, along with Bubble and Squeak and Miss Honeyberry. "Well?" the director of MICE-6 demanded.

The lab mouse who was examining the whisker looked up. He still clutched the magnifying glass in his paw, and he blinked at Sir Edmund through it, his pink eye disconcertingly huge. "There's no doubt about it," he announced.

"No doubt about what?" barked Sir Edmund.

The lab mouse cleared his throat. "The classification," he squeaked. "It's a rat whisker."

A collective gasp went up from the other mice.

"You're sure?" said Sir Edmund.

The lab mouse nodded. His huge pink eye nodded with him. "One hundred percent. It's a perfect match with these others we've collected in the past. Except of course for its color. I've never seen a gold whisker before. But the hue appears to have been painted on. Nail polish, most likely."

"How odd," said Sir Edmund. He turned to the field agents standing by the corkboard. "And how about you lot—have you come to any conclusions?"

The mice consulted their notes. "Definitely a mouseling," said one.

"Wasn't working alone," said another. "Some of the marks stumped us for a moment, but now that we know the whisker was a rat's, that explains it."

"Explains what?" said Sir Edmund irritably.

The field agent pointed to one of Glory's photos. "These marks here inside the ventilation duct," he said. "The ones that look like long swishes. We originally thought they were just where a bag with the jewels in it was dragged through the dust, but that's not it at all. They're tail marks. Rat tail marks."

"So we have a boogeyrat, not a boogeymouse," said Glory softly.

Sir Edmund clapped his paws together. "Miss Honeyberry, get me yesterday's surveillance footage from the

Tower of London," he ordered. "Our fly-spy cams must have caught something."

"Yes, sir," said Miss Honeyberry.

Glory cringed. She knew all about fly-spy cams; one of her own recent disasters had been caught on film and had temporarily cost her her job. But Sir Edmund was right. MICE-6's surveillance pilots were world-renowned for their diligence. If there were rats on the prowl, the cameras should have caught them.

"And I want to speak to Julius on the double," said Sir Edmund.

"Yes, sir," said Miss Honeyberry again and scurried from the lab.

Glory glanced at the clock. Her colleagues at the Spy Mice Agency would be well into their workday back in Washington. Miss Honeyberry returned, wheeling in a toy circus-train car. Glory frowned.

The lab mouse who had been examining the whisker scampered over. "My latest invention," he said proudly, opening the train-car door. He reached in and pulled out a sliding drawer. Atop it was propped a video-camera screen. A tiny lens was clipped to it, pointing straight toward them. A wire connected the screen to a foraged cell phone keypad, and an antenna stuck out from the back of it. "I call it the Video Scrambler. It's hot-wired to the building's satellite connection. Everything's encrypted, so we can't be overheard."

"Clever touch putting it on wheels, Z," said Sir Edmund.

The lab mouse looked pleased. "I thought you'd like

that. This way you can make calls from your office or the conference room—or even from here in the lab."

"Glory," said Bubble, "I don't think you and Z have been introduced yet."

"Your name is just Z?" said Glory to the lab mouse, surprised.

He bowed. "Short for Zirconium. My parents named my brothers and sisters and me after the periodic table of elements, starting with Actinium. 'We've got it covered from A to Z,' they like to tell everyone."

Squeak leaned over to Glory. "Remind you of anyone?" she whispered.

Glory smiled. Lab mice were a distinctive breed, no matter what their country of origin. Z was definitely Bunsen's opposite number—what spies called their counterparts in other country's agencies. "There's one thing I don't understand, though," she said to Z. "How will Washington be able to take our call?"

"I e-mailed the unit's specifications to the Spy Mice Agency several weeks ago," the pale white mouse replied. "It's been a joint Anglo-American project from the start. Very hush-hush, of course. This is our first chance to roll it out."

He turned to the keypad and tapped in the phone number for the Spy Mice Agency, then pressed the button for speaker mode. The sound of the phone ringing thousands of miles away in Washington filled the lab. Then the screen flickered, and Julius's face appeared.

"Morning, Glory!" he boomed.

Glory rolled her eyes. That was Fumble's old line. She

thought she'd heard the last of it, but apparently not. She spotted Bunsen standing behind her boss and waved. He waved back shyly.

Sir Edmund harrumphed and stepped in front of her. "We have a situation here, Julius," he reported. He held up the gold whisker and explained the circumstances surrounding its recovery.

"So you think this gold-whiskered rat is kidnapping street urchins?" said Julius. "And is likely the one responsible for the theft?"

Sir Edmund nodded.

Julius stroked the end of his tail thoughtfully. "But why would he make it look like Oz and D. B. took the Crown Jewels?"

The door to the laboratory flew open and Miss Honeyberry scurried in. She was clutching a sheaf of photos. "We found something," she said breathlessly, handing them to her boss. "Aerial shots of the Tower from yesterday. Look."

She plucked one of the photos from the stack and passed it to Sir Edmund. Glory, Bubble, and Squeak crowded round to get a closer look.

"It was taken yesterday afternoon, just before closing," said Miss Honeyberry. She tapped the photo with her paw. "There, down at the base of Traitors' Gate."

Four furry little heads drew together as the spy mice examined the photo. "Can you ask them to enlarge this?" asked Sir Edmund.

Miss Honeyberry passed him another photo. "I already did." The four heads drew together again.

"It's them," said Squeak. "I'd stake my skateboard on it."

"As would I," agreed Bubble.

"I'd know that ugly snout anywhere," said Glory grimly. She looked up at the camera. "Julius, it's Dupont. He's in London. With Stilton Piccadilly. They're here in this picture with the rat with the golden whiskers. The three of them are working together."

There was a long silence.

"That explains it, then," said Julius. "Revenge, rat-style."

Sir Edmund nodded soberly. "It would seem so."

"We have to find them!" cried Glory. "We have to get the Crown Jewels back, or Oz and D. B. will go to jail!"

"We have to find them first," said Bubble. "They haven't been anywhere near Piccadilly's lair—we've had it under surveillance 24/7 since he disappeared last month."

"True," said Sir Edmund.

"I have an idea," said Bunsen, ducking out of view.

"Where's he going?" said Sir Edmund as the lab mouse disappeared offscreen.

"I believe he means to check with A.M.I.," Julius replied.

"Amy?" Glory said, trying not to sound jealous. "Who's she?"

"Not a 'she,' my dear—a 'what,'" Julius informed her. "A.M.I. stands for 'Artificial Mouse Intelligence.' Your beau has built a computer. He's been keeping it under wraps at my orders."

Z gave a low whistle. "A computer! That's awesome!"

"And never fear, we're not holding out on our closest allies," Julius assured him. "We'll be sending you the specifications shortly. Bunsen just wanted to work the bugs out first."

Bunsen reappeared, towing his new invention. He fastened on the extra-strength helmet and clambered onto the keyboard. "I'm not very good at this yet," he said timidly. "In fact, I'm all paws. Not like you, Glory."

Before she became a field agent, Glory was a trained computer gymnast. She'd been plucked from the typing pool by Julius, who knew talent when he spotted it.

They all watched silently as Bunsen hopped slowly from one key to the next. "I'm Googling 'gold' and 'whiskers' and 'London,'" he shouted, breathing hard. "You never know—maybe we'll find something."

He halted, panting, and stared at A.M.I.'s screen. "Let's see . . . hmm . . . didn't turn up much. There's 'Golden Girls and White Whiskers'—"

Squeak waved her paw dismissively. "That's some silly play at a theater in the West End. I overheard the concierge at the Savoy talking about it. A lot of the elderly guests have booked tickets."

Bunsen peered at his computer again. "How about 'Goldilocks and Granny's Whiskers'? No, wait. That's a hair salon." He drooped slightly and slanted a glance at Glory. "Guess this wasn't such a good idea."

"Don't give up now, Bunsen," Glory encouraged. "Keep looking."

Her beau shrugged and scanned the screen, muttering

to himself as he hopped up and down "Nope, nope, nope," he said, scrolling through one entry after another. Finally, he paused. "Now that's an odd coincidence," he said.

"What?" said Sir Edmund.

"A certain D. G. Whiskers, Esquire, just placed an order at the Savoy for afternoon tea. The hamper is due to be delivered to his office in about an hour."

"What's so odd about that?" demanded the head of MICE-6.

Bunsen shrugged again. "The address is 80 Strand."

"That's right next to the Savoy!" said Squeak.

"Exactly," Bunsen replied. "The hotel where Oz and D. B. are staying. It just seems like an odd coincidence, that's all."

Sir Edmund stroked his tail thoughtfully. "It's a long shot."

"But worth a look, perhaps," said Julius. "Mr. Burner has a hunch, and I've learned in this business that sometimes it's best to go with one's hunches."

"Perhaps you're right," agreed Sir Edmund. "'Always trust your gut,' my great-grandfather used to say."

The mice were quiet for a long moment. Finally, Glory spoke up.

"I hear the Savoy has changed its menu," she said. "This year's Christmas Eve tea features scones with a side of spy mice. I'm going in."

CHAPTER 17

DAY TWO
DECEMBER 24
1600 HOURS

"I do not believe I am hearing this," said D. B. "Roquefort Dupont is *here*? In London?"

Oz couldn't believe it either. "But I thought—we all thought—"

"I know," said Squeak. "But it's true. The rats survived."

The three of them were in D. B.'s room at the hotel suite. Oz and D. B. had been kept under close guard since their interrogation by Scotland Yard. Although they had been released for lack of evidence, a dark cloud of suspicion hung over them. After the ransom note bearing Lavinia Levinson's fingerprints was received, the number of police watching them had doubled. Two officers were posted in the suite's living room. Two more stood outside the door in the hallway. And down in the Savoy's elegant lobby, there were no fewer than six plainclothes officers on duty. Scotland Yard was taking no chances.

Squeak was perched on Oz's knee, filling them in. "The *Mayflower* balloon went down in the North Sea," she explained. "The rats got lucky—a Norwegian fishing trawler picked it up. They stowed aboard, and now Stilton Piccadilly is back in town. He brought Dupont with him. Looks like they're working with another rat, an odd chap who paints his whiskers gold. We're pretty sure he's been kidnapping orphan mice and training them as jewel thieves."

Oz's mind was reeling. Dupont in London? A rat with golden whiskers who had a clutch of orphan mice—jewel thieves, no less—in his thrall? "Let me get this straight. Are you telling me you think that *mouselings* stole the Crown Jewels?"

Squeak nodded.

"And Dupont and the others made it look like we did it?"

"Glory's following a lead right now," said Squeak. "She and Bubble may have an answer for us soon."

"It's revenge, isn't it?" said Oz unhappily. "This is Dupont's way of getting even for what happened at Thanksgiving."

Squeak nodded again. "Rats don't like to be crossed."

"I suppose this would account for me feeling something brush past my ankles at the Tower last night," said Oz. "Remember, D. B.?"

D. B. jumped up off her chair. "Even if it's true, who's ever going to believe that a bunch of stupid rodents—excuse me, Squeak—were smart enough to snatch the Crown Jewels?" She shook her head, and her braids wagged sadly. "We're going down, Oz. We'll probably end up in a dungeon somewhere."

"Do they still stick people in dungeons?" cried Oz in alarm.

D. B. shrugged. "They probably make exceptions for people who steal crown jewels," she said gloomily.

Squeak looked over at the clock beside the bed. "I have to go, kids. I promised Sir Edmund I'd be back at headquarters in an hour. Busy day." She scooted down Oz's pant leg and picked up her skateboard.

"Wait, Squeak!" Oz pleaded, prodding anxiously at his glasses. "Scotland Yard took my CD player! I have no way of getting in touch if something happens at the concert tonight. If there even is a concert tonight," he added gloomily.

What with the ongoing investigation, it still hadn't been decided whether the Christmas Eve extravaganza at the Royal Opera House would proceed as planned.

D. B. crouched down on the carpet, placing herself at eye level with the British spy mouse. "What are we going to do about Priscilla Winterbottom? She's got something nasty up her sleeve—we just know it!"

Squeak sighed. "I'll keep a close watch on the news. If the concert isn't canceled, I'll try and stop by the opera house," she said. "But I can't promise anything. Sir Edmund may have other plans, and orders are orders." She mustered a smile. "But don't worry. You'll think of something."

Oz slumped in his chair. They were on their own, then.

Facing the worst shark in shark history. Not to mention Scotland Yard. D. B. was right—it was only a matter of time before they were all arrested.

Things couldn't possibly get any worse.

CHAPTER 18

DAY TWO
DECEMBER 24
1600 HOURS

"Mind the gap," squawked the large pigeon. He was perched on the roof of the imposing gray stone building that housed Churchill's wartime bunker and MICE-6.

Glory, who was about to climb aboard, paused. She looked around in bewilderment. "What gap?"

"Don't listen to Old Bart," said Bubble. "Just a habit he picked up in his youth. He was raised at Victoria Station, you see."

Glory didn't see at all, but she nodded anyway. Placing her paw in the paper-clip stirrup, she climbed aboard the pigeon's back. Bubble clambered up behind her.

"Old Bart's a bit featherbrained," he explained. "He probably should have been sent to a retirement roost ages ago, but the pilots have a soft spot for him. Plus, he's strong. They mostly use him for transport these days. He's the only pigeon on staff strong enough to carry the two of us and our gear."

MICE-6 was short-pawed and short-winged, as Sir Edmund had ordered every surveillance pilot aloft and every field agent out onto the streets in the hunt for Roquefort Dupont, Stilton Piccadilly, and the rat with the golden whiskers.

With a flap of his wings, Old Bart took off. He circled Parliament Square, gaining altitude, then headed northeast for the Strand and their teatime rendezvous at the office of D. G. Whiskers, Esquire. The sun was slanting low in the sky now, and the wind was cold. Glory shivered and nestled down farther into the big pigeon's feathers. Behind her, she could feel Bubble do the same.

Despite the cold and the wind, Glory couldn't resist poking her head out over the pigeon's wing and staring down at the city. At the rate her vacation was going, this short flight might be the closest thing she got to a tour of London. Below, the Thames gleamed dully in the late afternoon light.

"Here we are," said Bubble a short time later, as Old Bart swooshed past the clock on the side of number 80 Strand. "Largest clock face in London, by the way."

"Really?" said Glory, surprised. "Not Big Ben?"

Bubble shook his head. "Big Ben is more famous, but this one is bigger. And technically, Big Ben is the bell in the tower, not the clock."

"Interesting," said Glory as their pigeon alighted on the roof. She made a mental note to tell Bunsen. He'd want to know that.

"Mind the gap," said Old Bart again as Glory and Bubble slid down off his back.

"We always do," replied Bubble politely. He tapped the bird's tail feathers. "Don't wander off, now; we'll be back shortly."

"Mind the gap," repeated Old Bart automatically, bobbing his head.

Glory stooped down and opened her backpack. Beside her, Bubble did the same. They pulled out their silver skateboards and jammed on their bottle-cap helmets. Glory's pulse began to quicken, just as it did before every mission. Bunsen had not been happy with her volunteering for this particular one.

"Not *again*!" he'd cried, right over the Video Scrambler for everyone to hear. "Glory, are you completely nuts?"

But Glory had stuck to her guns. She was used to Bunsen's fussing. If her beau had his way, she'd be wrapped in cotton wool and kept in a safe. Besides, it made sense. She was the most experienced member of the team. She'd gone paw to paw with Dupont twice before. And if this D. G. Whiskers, Esquire turned out to be the rat they were looking for, it was only fair to everyone involved that the mouse with the most experience be there on the front line.

Squeak had lobbied hard to be included. "I know that building like the back of my paw," she'd argued. "My cousin is an editor for Tiny Tails—you know, the Publishing Guild? Those books for mouselings? Her office is under the sixth floor."

In the end, Sir Edmund had chosen Bubble instead. "I need you to debrief the children," he'd told a disappointed Squeak.

Glory looked over at Bubble. He gave a sharp nod, and the two of them zoomed off across the roof. The British spy mouse ollied up and into a ventilation shaft. Glory followed, and in a flash they were carving their way down the metal ductwork into the heart of the building.

"This is it!" called Bubble, spinning to a halt by a grate overlooking a long hallway. The mice tucked their Popsicle-stick boards into their backpacks and peeped out cautiously.

"There's his office, right across from us!" said Glory, spotting the glass door with D. G. WHISKERS, ESQUIRE etched on it.

Bubble poked his head through the grating and craned his neck toward the elevator. He checked the time on the face of the foraged wristwatch he had strapped across his chest for the mission. "Delivery boy should be along any time now. Shall we jump for it?"

Glory nodded. "We'll need a diversion, though," she warned.

"I've got just the thing," replied Bubble, rummaging in his backpack. "Z sent it along—thought it might come in handy." He pulled out what looked like a large rubber spider on a string.

"What is it?" asked Glory.

"A large rubber spider on a string."

"I can see that, for Pete's sake. But what does it do?"

"Scares humans," said Bubble.

"So it explodes?"

Bubble shook his head.

"Smoke bomb?" ventured Glory.

"Much more low-tech than that, I'm afraid," Bubble replied. "But effective nevertheless. You'll see." He tied one end of the string to the grating and crouched down, clutching the spider in his paws. Glory crouched down beside him. A minute later there was a loud *DING*, and they heard the elevator doors slide open.

"Here he comes," whispered Glory.

The Savoy's delivery boy sauntered down the hallway, whistling a Christmas carol. His eyes lit up when he spotted the envelope containing his tip by the panel in the wall. As he passed the ventilation grate, Bubble gave a mighty heave and launched the spider toward him. It landed on the delivery boy's shoulder. The boy shrieked, nearly dropping the tea hamper that he was carrying. He swatted at the rubber spider in a panic. This simply sent it swinging away again and then back at him, like a small black insect boomerang.

Glory and Bubble waited until one of the human's wild gyrations brought the basket under the grating. Then they made a leap for it.

"Agents in place," Bubble whispered a moment later into the tiny microphone clipped to his gray fur, as they ducked under the basket's lid.

"Smells wonderful," whispered Glory, sniffing the tea hamper's contents.

"The Savoy does a splendid tea," agreed Bubble. "My grandmother took me there once for my birthday." He inspected the treats. "Let's see, we've got scones with Devonshire cream and strawberry jam, cucumber sandwiches, petit fours, shortbread, and strawberries dipped in chocolate. Oh, and tiny Christmas puddings—how festive! And a thermos filled, I presume, with piping hot tea."

Glory was suddenly starving. Her stomach growled. Had she eaten lunch? She couldn't remember. It had been an intensely busy day. The hamper gave a thump as the delivery boy set it on the floor and rang the buzzer above.

Bubble tapped his transmitter, frowning. "This doesn't seem to be working," he whispered. "I'm not getting anything back from MICE-Six."

"Shall we proceed as planned?" asked Glory. "I'd hate to bail out when we're this close."

"Sir Edmund won't like it," said Bubble. "He's a stickler for protocol, and protocol says to scratch a mission if communication is disabled. But I agree with you, Glory." He tapped his tiny microphone again. "Maybe the malfunction is just temporary," he said hopefully. "HQ will probably come back online any second now."

Glory glanced around. "We'd better take cover in the meantime. We'll have to split up—there isn't much room in here."

Bubble pointed to a napkin at the bottom of the basket. "You take that," he said. "It's the safest spot. Rats aren't much for napkins."

Glory's stomach growled again. She shook her head and scampered over instead to a pile of scones on a china plate. "Napkin's all yours, Bubble," she said, taking a bite from a pastry at the bottom of the stack. "I'm going to hollow out this baby. Not even Roquefort Dupont himself could eat all these scones."

As her British colleague wiggled out of view, Glory took another bite. Suddenly, the tea hamper lurched forward and rose into the air. Glory toppled over, nearly landing in the dish of Devonshire cream.

"Whoa!" she cried softly. "Where are we going?"

Bubble poked his nose out from under the napkin and peered through the tea hamper's woven side. "I have no idea," he reported. "We're in an office, but apparently we're headed for the ceiling." He withdrew again, and Glory burrowed farther into her scone hiding place, munching as fast as she could.

A moment later the basket gave another thud as it settled on the floor.

"Ah, teatime," said a voice. A deep, melodious voice.

Glory nestled farther into the heart of her scone, whisking her tail safely out of view. The voice must belong to D. G. Whiskers, Esquire, but she couldn't tell by listening whether he was a rat or a human. Was this a wild goose chase? What if D. G. Whiskers, Esquire, was just some weird businessman who liked to have tea in his attic? But then again, what if he was the rat with the golden whiskers? Her pulse began to quicken. She'd scoffed at Bunsen's concern for her, but maybe her sweetheart was right. Maybe she was foolish to keep volunteering for these missions. What else could she have done, though? Oz and D. B.'s freedom was at stake. Surely rescuing one's friends was worth any risk, even a run-in with rats.

Above her, the lid to the basket creaked open.

"So what's on the menu today, Goldwhiskers?"

Glory's heart nearly stopped. Bunsen's hunch was right. There was no mistaking that voice. Roquefort Dupont's distinctive growl sounded like bolts in a blender.

"Oh look—wee Christmas puddings!" said Stilton Piccadilly. "I haven't had those since—"

"Since we went on that holiday outing as ratlings? Dumpster diving behind our fair city's hotels?" reminisced the deep, melodious voice.

So D. G. Whiskers, Esquire—aka Goldwhiskers—is definitely a rat, then, thought Glory.

"I ordered them as a special treat," continued Goldwhiskers. "For old times' sake, eh, Stilton? And to celebrate Operation S.M.A.S.H. Which stands for what, mouselings?"

"Stop Mice and Stop Humans!" Glory heard a host of little voices pipe in unison.

"And how are we going to accomplish that?"

"Incriminate, exterminate!" chorused the mouselings.

Exterminate? thought Glory in a panic. Incriminate was well underway, what with Oz and D. B. under suspicion, but exterminate? Were the rats planning more than just a jewelry heist, then? MICE-6 had to be told about this new development right away! But how, without a transmitter?

"Exactly," said Goldwhiskers to the mouselings. "Well done. Master is pleased with you. Master has food for you."

"Master, giver of all that is good!" chanted the mouselings, and Glory heard a scrabbling of tiny paws as the orphans scampered closer to the basket.

"Tut-tut!" said Goldwhiskers. "Mind your manners. Wait for Dodge."

There was a scraping sound as someone—*Dodge, presumably*, thought Glory—scaled the outside of the tea hamper, then landed with a small thump on the plate containing the scones. Glory hardly dared breathe. She strained to hear the trio of rats as they discussed Operation S.M.A.S.H.

"I can hardly wait until tomorrow!" chortled Stilton Piccadilly. "The mice won't know what hit them!"

"The terror-rats of London town, that's what!" crowed Dupont.

Glory shivered. She thought of what her father, the brave field mouse General Dumbarton Goldenleaf, had told her long ago. "Fear is a rat's best weapon," he'd said. Just as calm, cool, collected thinking was hers.

As the rats continued to boast, Glory's fear turned to fury. If she had anything to say about it, Operation S.M.A.S.H. would be turned into Operation M.A.S.H. instead: "Mice and Short Humans," teamed against the rats, not the other way around.

As the confections were lifted out and distributed to the

waiting rats and orphans, Glory could hear excited mur-murings and the smacking of rodent lips.

"Does it smell like mice in here to you?" Dupont asked suspiciously. Glory froze. Roquefort Dupont had a nose like a bloodhound.

"Well of course it does, you dolt," snapped Piccadilly. "We're nearly overrun with mouselings. Not to mention that vile pet of yours. Who smells dreadful, by the way."

"He's not my pet; he's my slave," said Dupont, sound-ing peeved.

"Whatever. You should give him a bath. He reeks of herring."

"I thought for a moment I caught a whiff of—never mind," grumbled Dupont. "Impossible. Throw me one of those cucumber sandwiches."

For a few minutes all that could be heard was the enthu-siastic crunching and slurping and burping that accompa-nied a rat feast. Glory wrinkled her nose in disgust. Rats were so revolting.

"Now that you've learned to read, perhaps it's time to learn some manners," Goldwhiskers said disapprovingly.

"Well, la-de-da and pardon me," said Piccadilly. "Sewer manners always used to be good enough for you, Double G."

"Anybody want this last scone?" Dupont asked. Not waiting for the others to reply, he whisked it out of the tea hamper.

Inside the pastry, Glory clutched desperately for a pawhold. *Oh, no!* she thought wildly, as the scone tumbled

onto the carpet. A second later she heard Dupont attack it hungrily, snuffling and gnawing at it. She recoiled in terror as his long, scabby snout broke through to her hiding place. As his razor-sharp teeth snapped closer and closer, she scrunched up into a tiny ball.

Suddenly, the snout withdrew. Glory looked around frantically for an escape route. There was none.

A fiery red eye appeared in the hole in the side of the scone. It widened when it spotted her. "Well, well, well," Dupont growled softly. "What have we here? Looks like Santa Claws brought my present a day early."

CHAPTER 19

DAY TWO
DECEMBER 24
1730 HOURS

Oz glanced over at Priscilla Winterbottom. Thanks to a royal reprieve—the queen was a big fan of Lavinia Levinson's and willing to give her the benefit of the doubt until proven guilty—the Christmas Eve concert was going forward as planned. Oz and D. B. and Priscilla, along with Luigi Levinson and a pair of policemen, were seated in the front row at the Royal Opera House watching the two sopranos warm up for the evening's concert.

Oz squirmed in his red velvet seat. Priscilla was looking far too pleased with herself. Oz knew that expression well. He'd seen it on the faces of countless sharks over the years, right before they attacked. She was definitely up to something. He just wished he knew what it was.

The theft of the Crown Jewels had given her an advantage, of course. She was only too happy to rub his and D. B.'s noses in the fact that they were the prime suspects.

"Guess this is the last concert your mum will sing for a while, huh?" gloated Priscilla.

"Shut up," said Oz.

Priscilla coughed. "They have special jails over here for kids like you, you know," she continued, ignoring him. She fished a hankie out of her purse and wiped her nose. "Nasty places with spiders and beetles. They don't give you any blankets, and there's nothing but moldy bread and cheese to eat. You'll never get to see your mum and dad, either."

Oz's father glanced over at them, and Oz thought he saw a flicker of sympathy in his eyes. But he didn't say anything.

D. B. scowled. "Mind your own business, Slushbutt."

"Or what?" taunted Priscilla Winterbottom. "Or you'll steal my mother's jewels, too?"

She whipped around, ferretlike, as Nigel Henshaw approached. Just as the younger boy reached the aisle seat where she was sitting, Priscilla stuck out her foot. He tripped and fell, banging his elbow against one of the seat backs. Nigel let out a yowl of pain, and his father threw down his baton in exasperation. The music ground to a halt.

"Didn't I remind you right before rehearsal to keep quiet?"

"But she—" the boy protested, pointing at Priscilla, whose hands were folded primly in her lap, the picture of innocence. *Just like a shark*, thought Oz in disgust.

"I'm sorry, son, but you'll have to stay backstage," said

Mr. Henshaw, tapping his baton impatiently on his music stand. "We can't have interruptions out here. The musicians need to concentrate. Go to my dressing room and stay there."

Cradling his wounded elbow, Nigel ducked his head in embarrassment and turned to go. As he passed Priscilla's seat, she discreetly stuck out her tongue. Then she coughed again.

Prudence Winterbottom stepped forward. She peered over the floodlights, shading her eyes with her hand. "Priscilla?" she called, sounding worried. "Is that you? You're not coming down with something, are you?"

Priscilla shook her head, sneezing, and blew her nose vigorously into her hankie.

"Can't have you honking like a goose during the concert, darling," said her mother. "I'll round up some cough syrup for you. There's some in my dressing room."

"I hate cough syrup," Priscilla whined. "It makes me sleepy."

"That's better than sneezy," replied her mother.

"How about Grumpy and Dopey?" whispered Oz to D. B., who stifled a giggle.

Prudence Winterbottom took her place onstage again, and the music picked up where it left off. Oz recognized the opening chords to "White Christmas."

"Cue fog!" the stage manager called out. "Cue boxes!"

As if by magic, a pair of enormous boxes gaily wrapped in shiny foil and topped with huge bows rose through the stage floor. Lavinia Levinson took a seat on the red one; Prudence Winterbottom sat down on the silver one. The two sopranos tilted their heads toward each other and began to sing.

"Brava!" cheered Luigi Levinson when they finished. The two divas stood up and took a bow, smiling at him. The presents they had been sitting on slowly descended again beneath the stage.

Oz jumped as D. B. elbowed him in the side. "What's Slushbutt up to?" she said.

Oz looked over to see the British soprano's daughter heading toward the lobby.

"I don't know. Let's see if we can find out," Oz whispered back. He turned to the policeman beside him. "Sir? I need to use the restroom."

"Me too," said D. B.

"I'll take them, Simon," said the other policeman, rising to his feet. He herded them out to the lobby. Oz caught a flash of blue from Priscilla Winterbottom's dress as she disappeared down a nearby corridor.

"Be quick about it," said the policeman, heading toward his colleagues, who were clustered by the entrance to the opera house. "And remember, I've got my eye on you."

"This way," said Oz, pulling D. B. down the corridor where Priscilla had disappeared. He glanced over his shoulder. The policemen were already deep in conversation. Instead of ducking into the restrooms, Oz and D. B. continued on down the corridor. Way at the end was a door marked BACKSTAGE. They watched as Priscilla pushed it open and walked through.

"Where's she going?" asked D. B.

"Probably thought of another way to make Nigel's life miserable," said Oz.

"You don't think she's just getting cough syrup? Or another hankie?"

Oz shot her a look. "Please. This is Slushbutt we're talking about, remember?" Looking back over his shoulder again—no policemen in sight—Oz darted through the backstage door.

"How will we ever find her?" said D. B. as she stared at the maze of corridors and stairwells that made up the behind-the-scenes world of the Royal Opera House.

"My mother's a diva, remember?" said Oz, steering her confidently along. "I grew up backstage. Ha! I knew it. There she is!"

They hung back and watched as Priscilla Winterbottom passed right by the conductor's dressing room and disappeared through another door beyond. Oz frowned.

"It's not Nigel she's after, then," said D. B. "Where does that door go?"

"Underneath the stage," replied Oz, sounding puzzled.

"Why is she going down there?"

"Beats me."

They followed, ducking behind a large crate marked AIDA ELEPHANT when she finally came to a stop. A few yards away in the understage gloom, Priscilla Winterbottom glanced around furtively. Satisfied that no one was watching, she tiptoed over to where the two giant presents that had been onstage just a few moments before were resting on the hydraulic platform that carried them up and down. Priscilla opened a large chest that stood on the floor nearby and took out a small package wrapped in newspaper. Then she slid open the back of the box wrapped in red foil.

"Isn't that the one your mom was sitting on?" whispered D. B.

Oz nodded. He frowned as Priscilla placed the newspaper-wrapped package inside the big box, then slid the back of it closed again. Looking around once more, she ran back toward the stairway. Oz and D. B. held their breath as she passed their hiding place.

"What the heck was that all about?" asked D. B. after she was gone.

Oz stood up and crossed to the chest. It was insulated, just like the one his dad used when he took him on fishing trips. He lifted the lid. His eyes widened. "Dry ice," he said in surprise.

"Dry what?"

"Ice. It's used in theaters all the time. It makes fog onstage. The stage manager must be planning to use it for the finale. To make it look like winter."

"Yeah, I heard her say, 'Cue fog!' But what would Slushbutt want dry ice for?"

Oz pushed at his glasses. He looked at the ice chest,

then at the foil-wrapped present his mother had been sitting on. He reached over and tapped the huge box. It gave a metallic ring. He groaned.

"I can't believe she'd do this!"

"Do what?"

"Don't you get it? This box is made of metal, D. B. Dry ice will freeze it in nothing flat. The sequins on my mother's dress will stick to it when she sits down!"

"Like last week, after the snowstorm, when Jordan and Tank made you lick the metal swing-set pole on the playground?" said D. B.

"Thanks for reminding me," Oz replied, reddening. "But yes, exactly."

"And when she goes to stand up at the very end and take her bow . . . ," said D. B. slowly, putting two and two together.

"Either she'll be stuck or the bottom half of her dress won't come with her," said Oz. "She'll be standing onstage in her underwear. In front of the queen!"

"Priscilla Winterbottom is a weasel!" said D. B. angrily.

"Shark," corrected Oz. "And a saboteur, to boot." He opened the back of the present and removed the small newspaper-wrapped package.

"A what?"

"Saboteur. Like sabotage, you know? Someone who damages something deliberately, or destroys somebody's efforts. I learned about it at the—"

"Spy Museum," finished D. B. "Should have known."

She placed her hands on her hips. "So Slushbutt thought she was going to give your mom a real 'winterbottom,' did she? Well, she's got another think coming. I'm going to march right upstairs and tell the police."

Oz grabbed her arm. "No, D. B. Wait. We can't let Priscilla know that we discovered her plan. She'll just come up with something else if we do. Something even more horrible. We've got to pretend we're completely clueless."

D. B. crossed her arms over her chest and frowned. "I don't like the sound of that."

Oz gave her a conspiratorial smile. "The thing is, we're not clueless. And I think maybe there's a way to turn the tables." He dropped the newspaper-wrapped package back into the insulated freezer chest, closed the lid, then pointed to the crate where they'd been hiding. "That gave me an idea."

D. B. looked over at it. She read the label and sighed. "Let me guess," she snapped. "We get to dress up, and I get stuck being the back end of an elephant this time. Forget it, Oz! I've had enough of costumes."

Oz's smile widened to a grin. "Not an elephant, D. B., and this time we won't be the ones wearing the costume, I promise. Come on, we have to find Nigel. We're going to need his help."

CHAPTER 20

DAY TWO
DECEMBER 24
1730 HOURS

"You'll never get away with this," said Glory calmly. Dupont had her by the tail and was dangling her upside down in front of Goldwhiskers and Stilton Piccadilly. "The building is surrounded."

Goldwhiskers looked down at her from his red-leather chair. "Is that so?" he sneered. "Let's take a look, shall we?" He tapped a series of commands onto his laptop keyboard, and the screen on the wall flickered to life. An array of security cameras zoomed in on 80 Strand from every possible angle, showing nothing but humans, cars, buses, and the rest of the normal traffic that clogged the busy street. The view was equally normal at the back entrance by Embankment Gardens. "Hmmmm. Not a mouse—let alone a Royal Guard—in sight. Are you sure about that?"

"She's lying," snarled Dupont. "I'd stake my tail on it."

Goldwhiskers regarded Glory speculatively. "That may well be, but I'll give her points for nerve. She certainly has guts, for a mouse. Put her down for a minute, would you, Dupont?"

Dupont growled reluctantly, gave Glory a hard shake, then released his grasp. She fell to the floor with a thud. Glory lay there for a few seconds, pretending to be stunned, while she tried to gather her wits. She was in a tight spot. The tightest, perhaps, that she had ever been in. Trapped in a room with two of the worst rats in history, plus one wild card: this D. G. Whiskers, Esquire, or Goldwhiskers. She tried not to think about the fact that she might not make it out alive. *Stiffen your tail, Goldenleaf,* she told herself. *You're a Silver Skateboard agent, and you have a job to do.* She picked herself up slowly and brushed off her soft brown fur. She had to stall for time. That at least might give Bubble a chance to escape.

One thing was clear: Goldwhiskers was the rat in control here. Glory smiled up at him. "The name is Goldenleaf," she said coolly. "Morning Glory Goldenleaf."

"James Bond fan, are we?" replied the big rat with a soft chuckle. "Playing at spy games?" He leaned down from his red-leather chair. "You know what happens to spies that get caught, don't you?" He drew one sharp claw across his throat.

Glory swallowed nervously. She glanced around the richly appointed room. Dozens of mouselings clustered along the walls, staring at her wide-eyed. She spotted Fumble, half hidden behind Dupont.

"What, no 'Morning, Glory'?" she asked her former

colleague scornfully. "What's the matter, rat got your tongue? Is this what you've sunk to, then, Fumble—exploiting innocent mouselings for some greedy windbag? Looks like you and Dupont have been on a diet, too." Glory wrinkled her nose and sniffed the air. "Fish, huh? Peeee-eeeeew. I suppose I should say, 'I smell a traitor!'"

Fumble stared at her defiantly for a few seconds. Then his gaze faltered, and he slumped onto the carpet. Glory turned back to Goldwhiskers. "The jig is up, Goldwhiskers," she said. "We know all about the Crown Jewels. And the kidnappings, and all the other robberies. You can't get away with it."

"Oh can't I? Watch me," Goldwhiskers replied, stroking the Koh-i-Noor. He looked over at Dupont and Piccadilly. "She's got spirit. I like that in a mouse. And she's amusing. Much more amusing than you two." He turned back to Glory. "Tell me, Miss Goldenleaf—I love your name, by the way—what would it take for you to come work for me?" He reached out a paw, and Dodge rummaged through the lacquered box on the table beside him. She pulled out a diamond bracelet and handed it to Goldwhiskers. He dangled it in front of Glory.

Glory's mouth dropped open. She couldn't believe her ears. Goldwhiskers was trying to bribe her!

"I'll triple your current salary," he offered. "Room and board included, plenty of holiday time. Plus I offer a generous retirement plan."

"She'll never do it," sneered Dupont.

"If I want your opinion, I'll ask for it," snapped Goldwhiskers. The big rat leaned down and draped the bracelet around Glory's neck. "I'll bet you don't see the likes of these on what the Spy Mice Agency pays you," he whispered silkily. "Diamonds are forever, or haven't you heard?"

Glory stroked the strand of sparkling jewels and flashed him her most flirtatious Mata Furry smile. She crooked her paw at him, and Goldwhiskers glanced over at Dupont triumphantly. He leaned down closer to Glory.

"You want me to be a Fumble?" Glory murmured.

"Hardly," Goldwhiskers murmured back in reply. "I'm offering you employment, not slavery. And I'd never keep you on a leash, I promise. Not even a diamond one. How about it?"

"How about . . . NEVER!" cried Glory, spitting in the big rat's eye.

"Told you so," said Dupont smugly.

Glory whipped the diamond bracelet from around her neck. "Diamonds are a mouse's best friend, or haven't *you* heard?" she retorted, looping it around Goldwhiskers's snout and giving it a sharp jerk. The big rat shrieked and toppled forward out of his chair. Glory leaped out of the way as he crashed to the floor.

She had to find a way to notify MICE-6 about the extermination plan! Quickly scaling the table, she raced to the telephone. She pretended to trip, then fell onto the speakerphone button. Glory danced rapidly across the keypad, just as she'd done as a computer gymnast, punching in the numbers for MICE-6's emergency line.

"Get her! Get that mouse! Defend Master!" screamed Goldwhiskers, frantically trying to untangle the bracelet, which was caught in his golden whiskers, and wipe the spit out of his beady red eye at the same time.

His frustrated bellows covered the sound of the phone ringing at MICE-6 headquarters. *Why don't they answer?* thought Glory. She only had a couple of seconds before she'd have to make a run for it.

Finally, she heard Miss Honeyberry's voice. "MICE-Six here," she said.

"DEFEND MASTER!" screamed Goldwhiskers simultaneously.

All around the cubbyhole, the mouselings drew back in confusion. Something was wrong. Terribly wrong. Their ears told them to defend Master, but their noses told them that Glory was one of their own. Instinct battled training. Instinct won out. They didn't move.

Dupont did, however. Before Glory could say a word to Miss Honeyberry, her arch enemy lunged for the table. Glory abandoned the phone and dove headfirst toward the carpet below, somersaulted three times, then sprang up and ran for the trapdoor. Dupont lunged again, grabbing her tail in his mangy paw.

"You won't get away this time," he snarled.

Glory twisted frantically in his iron-tight grip, but Dupont held her fast. He hoisted her up in front of his hideous snout. The stench of his breath was almost unbear-able. Glory's eyes began to water. She glanced over at the table as her archenemy bared his fangs in triumph. She had to warn her colleagues now!

Glory drew a deep breath. The next words she uttered might well be her last. "OPERATION S.M.A.S.H. UNDER-WAY!" she screamed with all her might, as Dupont swung her around his head like a lasso. "STOP MICE AND STOP HUMANS! GOLDWHISKERS AND THE OTHER RATS ARE PLANNING TO—"

Before Glory could finish her warning, Roquefort Dupont, whose ferocious whirling had sent them both spi-raling violently around Goldwhiskers's lair, tripped over the phone cord and yanked it out of the wall.

"No!" cried Glory, but it was too late. Dupont gave her tail one final savage twirl and flung her loose. She hurtled through the air like a tiny missile, narrowly missing a cluster of terrified mouselings. Glory landed on the floor with a crash and went limp.

CHAPTER 21

DAY TWO
DECEMBER 24
1800 HOURS

"One thousand extermina-
tors!" cried Bunsen. He stared at
A.M.I.'s screen, aghast.

Three thousand miles away, in
London, Sir Edmund Hazelnut-
Cadbury watched him on the Video Scrambler. Dozens of
mice peered over his shoulder. The staff at MICE-6 had been
on full alert since Glory's call had come through, and Sir
Edmund's office was jammed. "What was that, Mr. Burner?"
he demanded.

"I said, ONE THOUSAND EXTERMINATORS!" Bunsen
repeated, turning to face him. "This was what Glory was
trying to tell us!" He tapped the computer screen behind
him in agitation. "See? It's right here. I found a credit card
registered to D. G. Whiskers, Esquire—Goldwhiskers, as
Glory called him—and he used it less than an hour ago to
hire Rodent Rooter."

"Call Rodent Rooter!" sang one of the British computer
gymnasts automatically, and was quickly shushed.

"One thousand trucks, one thousand exterminators," continued the lab-mouse-turned-secret-agent. "They're scheduled to strike every neighborhood in the city at six a.m. tomorrow."

"On Christmas morning?" cried Z. "Ghastly!"

Sir Edmund nodded. "Ghastly, indeed," he said. "And coordinated attacks, no less. It's the Blitz all over again!"

"Can you cancel the exterminations?" asked Julius.

Bunsen shook his head regretfully. "Not without the security code on the back of Goldwhiskers's credit card," he said. "And even if we had that, we'd have to cancel by 2200 hours tonight. Rodent Rooter has an eight-hour cancellation policy. See?" He tapped A.M.I.'s screen again. "It's in the fine print here."

"Thank you, Mr. Burner," said Sir Edmund. "Your intelligence-gathering skills are remarkable. MICE-Six is in your debt."

Bunsen blushed modestly. Sir Edmund Hazelnut-Cadbury and Julius Folger stared soberly at each other via the Video Scrambler. Spymaster to spymaster, ally to ally, friend to friend, both of them contemplating the utter devastation that would follow such a vast number of coordinated attacks.

There was a worried buzz from the gathered mice, and Sir Edmund turned to face his staff. "This is a Code Red situation," he announced crisply. "We need that credit card. It's our only hope. I want 80 Strand surrounded ten minutes ago! Every mouse will do his duty. And hers. I want those rats stopped—and those orphans rescued—on the double."

"And Glory! Don't forget Glory!" added Bunsen anxiously.

"That goes without saying," snapped Sir Edmund. "Agent Westminster, too."

As his staff started to disperse, the head of MICE-6 held up his paw. "If the exterminations can't be canceled, we'll have to evacuate London."

There were more worried murmurs from the mice at this news. Never in mouse history—not even during the Blitz and the Great Turf War—had London's mice been evacuated. It was a daunting prospect.

"Do you have the mousepower to handle it?" Julius asked, his face on the Video Scrambler puckered with concern. "Not that there's anything I can do to help you at this point, Edmund, I'm afraid. Even if we sent agents and troops over on the next flight, they wouldn't arrive in time."

"Of course we can handle it," Sir Edmund replied stoutly. "We Londoners are made of stern stuff. We've faced down tyrants before, and we'll face them down again. Remember?" He pointed to the MICE-6 crest on the wall behind his desk and the words *Lux tenebras exstinguit.*

The gathered mice eyed their agency motto. Sir Edmund was offering them hope and courage and a reminder that other mice before them had faced dark times and come through. They sat up a little straighter.

"Miss Honeyberry, get on the phone to Buckingham

Palace!" ordered Sir Edmund. "We need authorization from the Prince of Tails to call in the Royal Guard. Call in the Welsh Rarebit Regiment while you're at it. We're going to need all the paws we can get."

A loud *whirr* and a *thwump* on the carpet announced the arrival of the Tube. Its hatch opened and Squeak popped out.

"Reporting for duty, sir," she said.

"Did you see the children?" asked Sir Edmund.

Squeak nodded. "I brought them up to speed, just as you asked," she reported. "I was listening to the news just now, and the concert has been given the green light. They're probably at the opera house already. But it doesn't look good, I'm afraid. Not with Lavinia Levinson's paw prints—I mean fingerprints—all over that ransom note. I expect they'll be arrested and officially charged the minute the concert is over. And they're very worried about Prudence Winterbottom's daughter. Apparently they think she's up to something."

"Nothing we can do about that now," said Sir Edmund regretfully. "There have been some new developments while you were gone. Alarming developments. I'm going to need you to lead a squadron of pigeons back to 80 Strand. With any luck, we should be able to save at least some of the orphans."

"Some?" cried Bunsen over the Video Scrambler, his nose and tail flaming bright pink with concern. "What about Glory?"

Sir Edmund sighed. "I promise you I haven't forgotten about Glory, Mr. Burner."

"A squadron won't be enough," said Julius. "If it were any other rats, perhaps. But not with Dupont and Piccadilly in the mix. And there must be dozens of orphans."

Sir Edmund tugged thoughtfully at his whiskers. He stared at the portraits on the wall. "What would Churchill and my great-grandfather have done, I wonder?" he mused. Suddenly, he spun about. "Julius," he said, addressing the Video Scrambler screen again. "I believe it's time to break out the Summoner."

Julius Folger was quiet for a long moment. "Are you sure?" he said finally. "It's an awfully big gamble. It was decommissioned more than half a century ago, after all. What makes you think they'll even respond?"

"Who will respond, sir, if you don't mind my asking?" said Squeak.

"It's a chance I'm willing to take," Sir Edmund replied to Julius, ignoring her. He turned to his staff. "Friends and colleagues," he announced. "I'm going to call in the S.A.S."

The room went dead silent. Not a tail twitched. Finally, one of the pilots cleared his throat. "The Secret Air Service?" he croaked.

Sir Edmund nodded. "Yes."

The mice exchanged nervous glances. The S.A.S. had long been rumored to exist, its exploits whispered of by the elders who'd been mouselings at the time of the Blitz and the Great Turf War. Ghosts, they were, said some. Swallows, said others. Swift as night, they'd swooped down from the skies of London, helping to turn the tide in the battle against the rats. And just as swiftly they'd disappeared, never to be seen or heard from since.

"I don't like the sound of this," said Bunsen anxiously.

"There's only one problem," continued Sir Edmund.

"What is that?" asked Julius.

"The Summoner," said Sir Edmund. "My great-grand-father entrusted it to his friend Winston Churchill after the wars were over. To keep it out of enemy paws. Churchill sewed it into the lining of his favorite waistcoat for safe-keeping, so my mother told me. That's what her father told her, and her father's father before him." Sir Edmund looked up at Julius again. "That waistcoat was donated to a museum after Churchill's death."

"Which museum?" asked Julius.

Sir Edmund turned to Squeak. "Cancel my original orders," he said. "I want you to go to the Royal Opera House instead. We're going to need the children's help."

CHAPTER 22

DAY TWO
DECEMBER 24
1800 HOURS

"Wait!" ordered Stilton Picca- dilly. Behind him, Goldwhiskers was scowling at his orphans.

Dupont's razor-sharp teeth stopped a whisker's width away from Glory's neck. He turned to the British bull rat. "Finders keepers," he snarled angrily. "She's mine."

"No, you fool, didn't you hear? She shouted something just before you knocked her out."

"So?" said Dupont, turning back to Glory, who had come to, but who had closed her eyes again in anticipation of her fate.

"Don't you understand?" shouted Piccadilly. "She was talking to someone! She was passing information about the exterminations!"

Dupont's beady red eyes narrowed. He pawed Glory's fur. "No transmitter," he reported, then gave her a brutal shake. "Are you working alone?"

Never give in, thought Glory bravely, remembering

Winston Churchill's rousing words. *Never give in. Never, never, never, never.* She gritted her teeth and kept silent, determined to protect Bubble no matter the consequences.

Dupont shook her again, more savagely this time. "Won't talk, eh? We'll see about that. I crack mice like nuts." He held up a razor-sharp claw and curled it around the base of her tail. Glory shivered. Dupont's thin rat lips peeled back in a hideous smile. "Still have a place for it on my wall, right beside your father's."

"For the love of garbage, Dupont," muttered Piccadilly, shouldering past him toward the tea hamper. "You always have to make such a production out of everything." He rummaged swiftly through the basket's contents, and gave a cry of triumph as he lifted the white napkin at the bottom. "Aha! Just as I thought." Reaching in, he plucked Bubble out by the scruff of his neck. "What did I tell you? They always work in teams. Double G! There's something you need to see."

Goldwhiskers was still glaring at his cowering mouselings. "Mouselings disobeyed Master," the big rat said in a low growl. "Mouselings didn't defend Master. What is wrong with *mouselings*?"

The orphans looked at one another in confusion. There was something new in Master's voice. Something they'd never heard before. And it was exceedingly unpleasant.

"Mouselings know what happens when mouselings defy Master!" Goldwhiskers continued, his voice rising to a deafening pitch. "Mouselings must be PUNISHED!" The orphan mice quailed. They clapped their paws over their ears. Goldwhiskers's voice dropped to a low hiss. "But this is *different*! This is *betrayal*! And betrayal calls for something *much, much* worse than the OUBLIETTE!"

Farthing squeaked in terror and climbed Twist like a tree. Twist wrapped his paws around the toddler and held him fast as the little one tried to burrow under his chin.

"Double G!" Piccadilly said again.

The big rat turned to Piccadilly. "What?" he snapped, breathing hard.

Piccadilly hoisted Bubble up in the air. "Your little friend wasn't working alone."

"So?"

"She called out a message, just before Dupont decked her. About the exterminations."

"He's probably got a transmitter," said Goldwhiskers.

Piccadilly turned Bubble upside down and shook him until his teeth rattled. Piccadilly's eyes narrowed. "I'm sure she was passing information, Double G. She ran up the table leg, remember, and then—"

Goldwhiskers whipped around and stared at the table by his red-leather chair. His gaze traveled up the table leg to the telephone that sat on its surface next to his gold-lacquered box. "You used my PHONE!" he screamed at Glory in outrage. "To transmit information about MY PLANS!"

Glory didn't say a word. *Never give in,* she told herself again. *Never, never, never, never.*

"Well transmit THIS!" Goldwhiskers cried. He whisked

the phone cord up in his huge paw, jammed it back into the plug in the wall, then smacked the speakerphone button and pressed redial. Glory could hear the phone ringing at MICE-6 headquarters, and then Miss Honeyberry's soft voice. "Yes?" she said anxiously. "Miss Goldenleaf, is that you?"

"How about Gold*whiskers* instead?" screamed Goldwhiskers. "You tamper with my world and my plans, you PAY! You want to play rat-and-mouse? You send your spy mice here to my home—to play I spy here in MY HOME? I'll send them back to you, and the orphans, too—if you can find all the PIECES, that is! And speaking of pieces, here's a little PUZZLE for you! I'm going to take all these DOUBLE-CROSSING, DISOBEDIENT, DISLOYAL mice on an outing tonight. A little Christmas Eve treat in London. Won't that be FUN?"

Glory, still held tightly in Dupont's grip, watched and listened as Goldwhiskers came unglued. She could hear it in his voice, just as she'd heard it in Dupont's before. It happened frequently when rats whipped themselves into a frenzy of retaliation. A very, very dangerous frenzy.

Goldwhiskers took a deep breath and chanted:

"Up on the rooftop the rodents pause,
Lots of mouselings in their claws.
Off for an evening of games and fun—
We'll come full circle when the night is done.
Round and round we'll go, then WHEE!
I'll be the last thing they ever SEE!"

The big rat's voice rose to a piercing crescendo. Behind him, the mouselings clutched each other in terror. Farthing let out a squeak of fear, and Goldwhiskers whirled around, pinning him with a ferocious glare. "Don't even THINK about it!" he roared, and slammed his paw down on the speakerphone button again, cutting off the call.

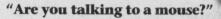

CHAPTER 23

DAY TWO
DECEMBER 24
1830 HOURS

"Are you talking to a mouse?"

Oz and D. B. started guiltily. Nigel Henshaw was standing at the door of Oz's mother's dressing room with an astonished look on his pale, pinched face.

"Uh," stammered Oz.

Nigel stared openmouthed at Squeak Savoy. She ducked under a large makeup brush on the dressing table, but it was too late. The damage was done.

Oz prodded nervously at his glasses. D. B. crossed her skinny arms across her chest. "What exactly do you think you saw?" she demanded.

Nigel pointed at Oz. "Him talking to that mouse," he replied. "The one hiding behind that brush there. And she was talking back to him. Said something about a secret mission, and him having to get out of here on the double."

What would James Bond do if he were here? Oz wondered desperately. Agent 007 was always wiggling out of tight situations. He was smart; he was wily; he was unflappable. At the moment, Oz did not feel the least bit smart or wily. And he felt extremely flappable. *The name is Levinson. Oz Levinson,* he reminded himself sternly. *Get a grip.* "Shut the door, Nigel," he said, as calmly as he could.

The younger boy shut the door.

"Um, Nigel," Oz continued. "D. B. and I couldn't help but notice the way Priscilla Winterbottom treats you."

Nigel's pale face flushed.

"How old are you, anyway?"

"Eight," Nigel mumbled.

"I'll bet you don't have many friends, do you?" said Oz gently.

Nigel shook his head miserably. His pale blue eyes filled with tears. Oz tried not to cringe. Looking at Nigel was like looking at himself a couple of years ago.

"Neither did I," said Oz. "But now I have lots of them. Do you know how?"

Nigel shook his head again. Oz leaned in close. "I became a secret agent," he whispered.

The boy's mouth dropped open in disbelief. Oz nodded. "That's right. I help my spy friends, and they help me. And they can help you, too. How would you like it if my friends and I fixed it so that Priscilla Winterbottom never bothered you again?"

Nigel brightened. "You could do that?"

"Uh-huh," said Oz. "You have to do something for us, too, though. You have to swear you'll do it, on your honor."

"On my honor," Nigel promised solemnly.

"You can never, ever tell anyone what you see here in this room tonight," said Oz.

Nigel nodded. "Okay."

D. B. elbowed Oz sharply. "This is a bad idea," she whispered.

"I know what I'm doing," Oz whispered back.

D. B. shrugged. "Have it your way."

"Squeak?" said Oz. "Come on out and meet Nigel Henshaw."

The bristles on the makeup brush parted and Squeak stepped out into the light. She looked nervous. So did Nigel.

"Remember those friends of mine I was telling you about? Well, Squeak is one of them, Nigel. And she's in trouble. Big trouble."

Nigel's eyes were as round as pennies. He looked from the mouse to Oz and back again.

"Hello," said Squeak.

Nigel managed a wave.

"Squeak, do you happen to have a MICE-Six badge?" asked Oz.

The mouse rummaged through her backpack, pulling out a tiny object and passing it to Oz. Like the Spy Mice Agency badge, it was round and very simple in design. But the MICE-6 crest was different: a candle against a navy blue background. *True-blue,* thought Oz. He read the inscription that encircled it haltingly. "'*Lux tenebras exstinguit.*' That's Latin, right?"

Squeak nodded.

"*Lux* is 'light,'" Nigel piped up. "I'm taking Latin at school."

"Very good, Nigel," said Squeak. "It means 'light extinguishes darkness.' That's the MICE-Six motto."

"And that's what you will help the brave mice of London do, from this time forward," said Oz, holding up the badge. "I hereby deputize you, Nigel Henshaw, as an honorary member of MICE-Six. Adjunct spy mouse and defender of mice against evil rats."

"Sir Edmund is going to kill you," muttered D. B.

Nigel looked at the three of them wonderingly.

"I'll explain more later," said Oz. "Right now, I need you to bring me something. Can you get into the wardrobe department's closets?"

Nigel nodded.

"Good. I saw the posters in the lobby for the *Nutcracker* ballet—it's being performed here this week, right?"

Nigel nodded again.

Oz scribbled something down on a slip of paper and handed it to his new colleague. "I need you to bring me this. Remember, it's for a good cause."

"Mice?" asked Nigel, shooting Squeak a shy glance.

"Priscilla," said Oz. "She's due for a rude awakening later tonight."

"We need to think of a way to make her go to sleep first, though," said D. B. "If that cough syrup doesn't do the trick."

"Chamomile tea always makes me sleepy," suggested Nigel. "My dad has some in his dressing room."

Oz looked over at D. B. "See?" he said with pride. "He's a natural." He turned to the younger boy. "Good thinking. You go get the tea and the stuff from the *Nutcracker* closet, and we'll wait right here for you. Oh, and don't let the policemen catch you! Remember, this is a top-secret mission!"

Nigel nodded, his eyes shining with excitement, and darted out of the dressing room.

"How am I going to explain this to Sir Edmund?" Squeak demanded.

"Desperate times call for desperate measures," Oz replied.

"Yes, but talking to another human is *really* desperate, Oz," said Squeak unhappily. "You and D. B. are an exception. I could lose my job for this."

D. B. reached out a finger and gently patted her shoulder. "Don't worry, Squeak. You can just say it's all Oz's fault if anything goes wrong."

"Thanks a bunch," said Oz.

"Well it is," D. B. retorted. "Wasn't my idea, that's for sure."

"So, how are we going to get you out of here, Oz?" asked Squeak. "Too bad you aren't smaller, or I'd lend you my board."

Oz looked at her Popsicle-stick skateboard and grinned. "I'm definitely too big for that."

D. B. picked up the makeup brush on Lavinia Levinson's dressing table. "I have an idea," she said. "Remember that workshop we took at the Spy Museum a couple of Saturdays ago? The one on disguises?"

Oz nodded.

"How about we disguise you as an old man?" said D. B. "You can wear your father's coat over your clothes, and maybe Nigel can find us a scarf and a hat somewhere. Too bad Scotland Yard took your grandpa shoes."

Oz stared down at his feet, which were now clad in black sneakers. "Even if you can pull it off, how am I going to get past the police guard?"

"We'll think of something," said D. B. "Sit down."

Oz sat, and while Squeak looked on, D. B. took a grease pencil and started drawing lines on his forehead and face. She worked swiftly and efficiently, and when she was done, she stood back and admired her handiwork. "Wrinkled as a prune," she said. "But take your glasses off. You'll never get past the police wearing those. They're a dead giveaway."

Oz took his glasses off. He blinked. Everything was blurry. "I can't see a thing," he said, starting to panic. What Sir Edmund was asking him to do was scary enough with twenty-twenty vision.

"I'll be with you the whole time," said Squeak. "I can be your eyes."

"Great," muttered Oz.

"Take a look," said D. B., when she was done.

"How?" Oz complained. "I can't see."

D. B. held a hand mirror two inches from his face. He peered into it. "Not bad," he said, turning this way and that. "I really look old. Amazing!"

"Thanks," said D. B.

"I wish we had a wig, though. I need some gray hair."

"A hat will work just fine," said Squeak. She looked at her watch. "We've got to get going. There's no time to lose if we're going to rescue the orphans and stop the exterminations."

There was a gentle tap on the door and Nigel entered. "Got it!" he said breathlessly, holding up what looked like a huge gray bath mat.

He stared at Oz and blinked.

"It's me, Nigel," Oz said. "I'm in disguise."

"Did the policeman see you?" asked D. B.

Nigel shook his head. "I pretended to go into my dad's dressing room, then waited until the guard was busy with his newspaper again."

Oz slapped him a high five. "Double-O-Nigel!" he said. "You're on your way to becoming a real secret agent!"

The younger boy's pale face flushed with pride.

"Any chance you can find us a scarf and a hat?" asked D. B.

"A gray wig and some size-ten shoes would be even better," added Oz.

"I'll see what I can do," said Nigel, and darted out again.

"Let's go over the plan," said Squeak. "We take the Tube to the museum first."

"The subway?" said D. B. "Cool."

"I tell the night watchman I lost my glasses," continued Oz, handing them reluctantly over to D. B., "and get him to let me in—"

"And we retrieve the Summoner," finished Squeak. "It's foolproof."

Oz grunted. Things were never foolproof. Especially when they involved him. "What if the night watchman doesn't answer the door, or won't let me in?"

Squeak shrugged. "We'll think of something. He's definitely on duty—the computer gymnasts already checked."

Oz shook his head. There were too many "what if's?" for comfort. "What does this Summoner look like, anyway?"

Squeak shrugged. "I haven't a clue. Nobody's ever seen it but Sir Peregrine Inkwell and Winston Churchill."

"Great," muttered Oz again.

"So while you head for the rendezvous, Nigel and I lure Prissy Slushbutt in here and see if we can put her to sleep," continued D. B. "I just hope she likes chamomile tea."

The door opened again and Nigel slipped in. He held up a ratty gray scarf and a matching wool cap in triumph. "These were in my dad's closet," he said. "Couldn't find a wig or shoes, though."

D. B. bundled Oz into his father's coat. It reached nearly to his ankles, and the arms were so long she had to turn the sleeves back three times before his hands appeared.

"How do I look?" said Oz.

"Like a demented old man playing dress up," said D. B.

She jammed the cap over his blond hair, then wound the scarf around his neck. She looked him over and sighed. "It will have to do. Just keep your chin down, stay in the shadows as much as possible, and don't stop for anything."

Squeak scrambled up the coat and somersaulted into its chest pocket. "Right, then," she said. "We're off."

"Wait!" cried D. B. "What do we do if the policeman comes in looking for Oz?"

Oz eyed Nigel, then passed him his tuxedo jacket. Nigel put it on. It reached below his knobby knees.

"Put my glasses on," Oz ordered, as D. B. handed them to the younger boy.

Nigel obliged. The result was ridiculous. The only similarity between the two boys was the fact that they were both fair-haired.

"I'll pad the coat to make him look fatter—I mean bigger," said D. B. hastily. "If he sits in the chair in the corner with the lights off, maybe we can fool the guard."

"We really must go," said Squeak. "Good luck, D. B."

"Good luck to you, too," D. B. replied.

"Thanks," said Oz. "We're going to need it."

CHAPTER 24

DAY TWO
DECEMBER 24
1300 HOURS

MICE-6 headquarters erupted in pandemonium as Goldwhiskers abruptly ended his phone call.

"They're on the move!" shouted Sir Edmund Hazelnut-Cadbury. "Mobilize the Royal Guard! Alert the surveillance pilots! *Save those mice!*"

Behind him, the videoconference screen was dark. The Scrambler's satellite feed had gone down, and Z was frantically trying to repair it.

"Have the gymnasts keep Washington updated by e-mail for now," Sir Edmund barked at his secretary. "And Miss Honeyberry?"

"Sir?"

"Fetch me the best cryptologist we've got. We need to solve that puzzle."

"He did mention 'up on the rooftop,' sir. One can't help but think of Santa's sleigh. And something about 'round and round we'll go'—perhaps he's referring to the rotor blade on a helicopter? We know he has a credit card—could he have hired one? There's a helipad on the roof of the Savoy."

Sir Edmund contemplated this suggestion. A rat with a credit card was a dangerous thing indeed. "Excellent thinking, Honeyberry," he said. Remind me to promote you. Hang on, scrub that, I need you right where you are. And get me Squeak Savoy on the transmitter. We'll need her expertise over at the hotel, if that's where the rats are heading. She's being recalled, effective immediately."

"But the human boy—"

"Ozymandias?" said Sir Edmund. He shook his head in regret. "He'll just have to go it alone."

CHAPTER 25

DAY TWO
DECEMBER 24
1945 HOURS

Oz shuffled down the hallway, hat pulled low over his forehead and eyes. The backstage corridor was dimly lit, thank goodness. He tried to remember the tips he'd learned in the workshop at the Spy Museum back home.

When in disguise, be your character. Act the part. Convince yourself, and you'll convince everyone around you.

Oz tried to imagine what it would feel like to be old. A hundred, say. He slumped a bit, and tried out a limp. Ahead sat the policeman, guarding the exit door. He was reading the paper. "American children interrogated in crown jewel affair!" screamed the headline on the front page. Oz winced. He paused in front of Prudence Winterbottom's dressing room. It was empty, he knew. The British soprano was already onstage with his mother. It was nearly eight o'clock, and the concert was about to begin. Oz knocked on the door.

The policeman looked up sharply. He saw Oz and frowned.

"Oi! Old-timer! No one's allowed back here!" he called.

"Just wanted an autograph," creaked Oz, hoping he sounded old and rusty.

The policeman stood up and opened the exit door. "Some other time, mate. Happy Christmas to you."

Oz shuffled past him, hardly daring to breathe. I am a hundred years old, he told himself. He could feel Squeak huddled in his coat pocket. If he was discovered now, it was all over. Caught trying to escape, they'd say, and throw him in the slammer. Or the dungeon at the Tower of London.

The exit door closed behind him, and Oz took a deep breath. So far, so good. He squinted at his surroundings. "Which way?" he whispered.

A furry head poked out of his pocket. Squeak took a quick look around. "Straight ahead," she said. "The Covent Garden station is the one you want. We'll take the Tube to Piccadilly Circus, then change trains for Baker Street. But we have to hurry. Can you go a little faster?"

"I'm trying to stay in character," Oz explained, but he dropped the limp as he stepped into the tide of last-minute holiday shoppers thronging the sidewalk. Dodging people and shopping bags as he was swept forward, he made his way to the Tube stop.

Oz bought a ticket, fed it into the slot, passed through the turnstile, and tottered toward the escalator into Covent Garden station. Down, down, down it whisked him and Squeak, deep into the heart of London's Underground, the vast subway system that served the city.

"Mind the gap," said an automated voice as Oz stepped onto the train. He peered down at his feet, taking care to avoid the crevice between the subway and the platform.

"Please, sir, take my seat," a girl about his age said politely, rising to her feet.

Oz started to protest, then caught himself. *You are a hundred years old, Levinson*, he reminded himself. He wheezed a thank-you and sat down as the subway train's doors closed. A few seconds later they were speeding out of the station.

Squeak poked her nose out of the coat pocket cautiously. "Festive," she remarked, nudging Oz.

Oz peered at the boy seated across from him. He was dressed in full punk garb, with a black leather jacket and matching studded collar, along with multiple piercings. His hair was spiked to an alarming height and dyed in alternating red and green stripes for the holidays. Oz grinned.

"Reminds me of the Steel Acorns," he whispered, referring to Glory's brother B-Nut's rock band back in Washington.

They got off at Piccadilly Circus—"where Stilton Piccadilly has his lair," Squeak informed him—and changed trains for the Bakerloo line. Three more stops and they reached their destination. Oz squinted his way through the underground corridors to the escalator, and they emerged into the London night.

"Faster, Oz!" urged Squeak.

Oz broke into a slow jog. After about a dozen paces, he

started to pant. Even if he wasn't a hundred years old, he still couldn't get anywhere faster. That was the problem with being fat. "Gotta slow down," he said breathlessly. "If I sweat, the makeup will smear."

"Hold on, Oz—I'm getting a transmission!" said Squeak.

Oz ducked gratefully into a doorway and leaned against the wall, sucking in lungfuls of air.

"Right," he heard Squeak say, along with a rapid scratching as she scribbled something down. "Got it."

"Got what?" asked Oz, as she climbed out of his pocket.

"New orders," said Squeak. "We have to split up."

"What?"

"That was Sir Edmund. I've been recalled from this mission," Squeak explained. "He's ordered me to proceed directly to the Savoy. They think the rats are headed for the helipad, and if that's the case, I know that rooftop like the back of my paw."

"You're going to just *leave me here*?" Oz's voice rose in panic. He looked around frantically. It was dark. He was in an unfamiliar city. And on top of that he couldn't see.

Squeak patted his shoulder. "You'll be fine, Oz. Remember how well you did in New York City? Like Glory says, you're true-blue. The museum's right over there, down the street. See? Madame Tussauds waxworks."

"I've heard of that," said Oz cautiously. "My dad promised to take me and D. B. there."

"Course he did," said Squeak. "All the American tourists go there. It's great fun. Or so I've heard. Never been there myself. She peered at the building. "Good—the light's on in the alley. That means the night watchman's on duty. Now all you need to do is get him to let you in."

"What if he won't?"

"He will. It's Christmas Eve—he'll be feeling generous. Tell him you need your glasses to watch your grandchildren open their presents. Once he turns his back, ditch him. Winston Churchill shouldn't be hard to find."

"It would help if I really did have my glasses," grumbled Oz.

He felt a small, furry paw pat his cheek. "Here," said Squeak, passing him a tiny penlight (foraged from a lost key chain). "This torch will help."

"This what?"

"Um, flashlight. That's what you Americans call them, right?"

Oz nodded glumly.

"And you'll need this to get the Summoner out of Churchill's waistcoat," she added, unhooking a tiny penknife from her utility belt and passing it to him. "Once you have the Summoner, proceed to St. Paul's Cathedral. I'm writing this all down for you. Baker Street to Oxford Circus, change to the Central line. St. Paul's is exactly four stops."

Oz's heart began to beat wildly as his tiny colleague handed him two teeny slips of paper. "This other note has the coordinates for the S.A.S.," she said. "Birds, from what I understand. Swallows of some sort. Tell them to meet us on the Savoy's rooftop for the orphan airlift."

Oz couldn't help it. His eyes filled with tears.

Squeak sighed. "Oz, I have to go," she said gently. "This is our darkest hour. Every mouse must do his or her duty, Sir Edmund told us, and that includes you, Agent Levinson. If we're going to pull off this rescue, and stop the exterminations, and save London, and get the Crown Jewels back, we need you! You do understand, don't you?"

Oz swallowed hard. He nodded and wiped his eyes.

"That's the spirit!" Squeak gave a sharp whistle, and a pigeon swooped low. She leaped nimbly onto her taxi's back. "Good luck, Oz!" And with that she flew off.

Oz stepped out of the doorway and looked around. Traffic whizzed by. Londoners rushed past him on the sidewalk in a steady stream, their arms loaded with Christmas packages. A group of carolers clustered beneath a nearby streetlight singing "God Rest Ye Merry Gentlemen." Oz didn't feel even remotely merry. He'd never felt so completely alone and scared in all his young life.

He turned the collar of his father's coat up against the sharp December wind and crossed the street toward the wax museum.

CHAPTER 26

DAY TWO
DECEMBER 24
2030 HOURS

"More chamomile tea, Priscilla?"

D. B. and Priscilla Winterbottom—
and Nigel Henshaw, who was not yet
dressed as Oz—were seated in Lavinia
Levinson's dressing room. Onstage, the
concert was well underway. The children had been
requested to stay backstage until after the intermission.
Easier for the police to keep track of that way, Scotland Yard
had decided. Priscilla Winterbottom was not happy to have
been included in this decision.

"Just a tad bit more," said Priscilla, holding out her cup.
"And I'll take another biscuit as well. It's the least you can
do, after all, considering I'm stuck back here thanks to you.
Where's Oz?"

"He's in the restroom," said D. B., filling her guest's cup
to the brim.

Priscilla took a few sips, ate a piece of shortbread, then
blew her nose into her hankie. "This is going to be an exciting evening," she said, smiling a sly ferret smile.

"Very exciting," agreed D. B., winking at Nigel.

The younger boy fingered the MICE-6 badge on the collar of his shirt.

"Haven't seen that before, Nigel," Priscilla said sharply. "Are you a jewel thief now as well?"

"Just a little souvenir I gave him," said D. B. smoothly.

Priscilla, who was filled to the brim with cough syrup and chamomile tea, yawned. Nigel bent down and pretended to tie his shoe, then reached over and turned up the heater. Squeak had suggested making the dressing room as warm as possible. "That always worked in our nest back home when I was a mouseling and mum wanted me to go to sleep," she'd advised.

Priscilla yawned again. "Too much excitement, I suppose," she said. "What with the Crown Jewels missing and all." She shot D. B. a smug look.

D. B. just smiled. She pretended to yawn. Priscilla yawned back. "I could use a nap—how about you?" D. B. said, patting the sofa cushions encouragingly. "It's been a long day. What with being at Scotland Yard all night and everything, I mean."

"I don't know how I'd be able to stand it, if I were you," said Priscilla, sipping more chamomile tea. "You might as well just confess. Everyone knows you did it. Scotland Yard knows it, the newspapers know it—everybody. You and Oz are nothing but common thieves. I shouldn't even be in here with you. Who knows what you might do?" She clutched the pearl necklace around her throat dramatically.

D. B. gritted her teeth and smiled politely. She pretended to yawn again. Priscilla yawned back and glanced longingly at the sofa. "Maybe I will just close my eyes for a minute. Nigel?" Her voice rose sharply.

"Yes?" the younger boy replied.

"Wake me at intermission," Priscilla ordered. "And don't forget. You know what will happen if you forget."

Nigel nodded unhappily. "Yes, Priscilla."

Priscilla Winterbottom stretched out on the sofa. D. B. quickly dimmed the lights. Nigel turned the heat up a bit more. As the girl's eyelids drooped, Nigel quietly pulled on Oz's tuxedo jacket. D. B. waited until Priscilla's breathing was deep and even, then began stuffing the chest and belly of the jacket with throw pillows from the chairs. When she was done, she placed Oz's glasses on Nigel's nose and sat him down in a chair in the corner farthest from the door. "There," she said. "You're Oz."

"He's not Oz," mumbled Priscilla sleepily.

There was a knock at the door. A policeman poked his head in. "Everything all right in here?"

"Just fine, officer," said D. B.

"Oz is in the loo," mumbled Priscilla, her eyelids fluttering in a vain attempt to open them.

"No he's not," said D. B. soothingly. "You were dreaming. He's right here. Nigel is in the restroom."

The policeman peered at the bulky figure in the corner. "You kids make sure you stay put this time," he said. "No funny business."

"No, sir," said D. B., as he withdrew.

"Let's hope Oz gets back here on the double," D. B. whispered to Nigel. "If he's not back by intermission, our goose is cooked."

"I love cooked goose," Priscilla murmured, and started to snore.

CHAPTER 27

DAY TWO
DECEMBER 24
2045 HOURS

"Any sign of them?" asked Squeak, hopping down off her pigeon's back.

"Not so much as a paw print," a Royal Guard replied. "A team of commandos just reported in, though—the office next door at 80 Strand is empty. Seems Goldwhiskers had a lair hidden in the attic above. It was empty too. They're definitely on the move."

Squeak peered over the edge of the Savoy's rooftop. She looked down the side of the hotel building to the street. She scanned the sky in all directions. "And you're sure this is where they're heading?" she said doubtfully.

The guard shrugged. "I'm just following orders. I hear there was some sort of a clue, or riddle. One of the whiz-whiskers down at MICE-Six decoded it and sent us here."

Squeak's ears perked up at this. "Clue? What clue?"

"Didn't they fill you in?"

Squeak shook her head. "We've been on kind of a tight schedule," she said. She pressed the button on the transmitter clipped to her fur. "Agent Savoy checking in."

"Ah, there you are, Squeak!" Sir Edmund replied. "Ozymandias is on his way?"

"Yes, sir," Squeak responded. "I understand there's something about a clue?"

"That's right. This Goldwhiskers, as he likes to call himself, is toying with us." Her boss sounded annoyed. Squeak heard a rustling of paper and Sir Edmund continued, "He said, and I quote, 'I'm going to take all these double-crossing, disobedient, disloyal mice on an outing tonight. A little Christmas Eve treat in London. Won't that be fun?' Then he finished with this riddle:

'Up on the rooftop the rodents pause,
Lots of mouselings in their claws.
Off for an evening of games and fun—
We'll come full circle when the night is done.
Round and round we'll go, then WHEE!
I'll be the last thing they ever SEE!'"

"That's it?" said Squeak.

"That's all of it."

Squeak was quiet for a moment. She gazed out across the Thames. It was a beautiful Christmas Eve, clear and cold. The sky was already alight with stars, and a full moon was rising. It was difficult to imagine that in just a couple of hours, unless they were able to stop it, the city would be under attack.

"'Round and round we'll go,'" she mused. Her gaze came to rest on the enormous Ferris wheel downriver from the hotel. "Oh, no," she whispered. "'Whee? Sir!"

"Yes?" Sir Edmund replied.

"Goldwhiskers wasn't talking about the Savoy at all!" cried Squeak, leaping back onto her pigeon. "He's taken Bubble and Glory and the orphans to the London Eye! We've given Oz the wrong coordinates for the S.A.S.!"

CHAPTER 28

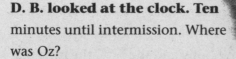

DAY TWO
DECEMBER 24
2050 HOURS

D. B. looked at the clock. Ten minutes until intermission. Where was Oz?

"We can't wait any longer," she said finally. "We've got to get this show on the road."

She stood up. Nigel heaved himself out of his chair and waddled over to join her.

"You can take off your Oz suit for now," said D. B., helping him unbutton the coat and remove the pillows. "I need you to be Nigel again."

"What are we going to do?"

"First, we need to get Slushbutt here into her costume."

Working quickly, the two of them bundled the sleeping Priscilla Winterbottom into the costume from the *Nutcracker* ballet's wardrobe. "There," said D. B., adjusting the hood. "Suits her to a tee." She looked around the room, frowning. "Now the question is, how do we get her past the policeman?"

"There's a big linen cart in the housekeeper's closet out-side," offered Nigel. "We could put her in that."

D. B. smiled. "You don't miss a trick, do you, kid? I think Oz may have been right about you."

The small, pale boy fingered his MICE-6 badge proudly and offered D. B. a shy smile in return.

"Think you can get that cart in here without the guard seeing?"

"I'll try." Nigel opened the door a sliver and peeked out into the hall. The policeman's back was turned; he was watching the concert from the stage wings. As the two sopranos swung into "The Holly and the Ivy," the tune that would close the first half of their Christmas program, the younger boy tiptoed to the housekeeper's closet, grabbed the linen cart, and wheeled it back to Lavinia Levinson's dressing room.

"Give me a hand, would you, Nigel?" whispered D. B., hoisting the sleeping form of Priscilla Winterbottom up off the sofa. The two of them managed to sling her gently—very gently—up and over the side of the cart, settling her onto a heap of soiled linens.

"Peee-eeeewww," said D. B. softly, wrinkling her nose as she climbed in beside the British soprano's daughter and burrowed beneath a towel.

"Yeah," agreed Nigel. "Those ballet dancers really work up a sweat."

"Can you get us to the elevator?" D. B. asked him, her voice muffled by dirty laundry.

In reply, Nigel Henshaw wheeled the cart quietly out of the dressing room. The guard's back was still turned. The younger boy pushed the cart slowly and carefully down the hall. Just as he passed the guard, Priscilla Winterbottom let out a snore. The policeman wheeled around.

"Stop!" he called.

Nigel halted, and the policeman eyed him suspiciously. "You're the conductor's son, right?"

Nigel nodded.

"I thought your dad told you to stay in his dressing room."

"Just until intermission," Nigel said meekly. "I'm taking these down to the laundry for housekeeping."

The detective glanced into the cart. "Whew," he said. "Stinky."

Nigel nodded in agreement. "The towels always need a good wash after the matinee. They weren't seen to today—housekeeper's off on holiday."

"Right then, lad. Nice of you to lend a hand. Off you go. Haven't been bothering those two American kids, have you?"

"Oh no, sir," said Nigel. He started forward with the cart again. It let out another snore, and Nigel coughed loudly to cover it. The guard frowned, but the haunting strains of the ancient carol drew him back, and with one last glance over his shoulder at Nigel he allowed his attention to be drawn back to the stage.

Nigel turned the corner of the hallway and broke into a

run. He screeched to a halt in front of the elevator, and a minute later they were in the basement.

D. B. climbed out of the laundry cart and slid open the back of the enormous silver foil-wrapped present on the hydraulic lift. "Be careful not to wake her," she whispered as she and Nigel wheeled the laundry cart up onto the platform and into the box. Priscilla squirmed restlessly for a moment, then settled in with a sleepy sigh.

"Can she breathe in there?" asked Nigel anxiously as D. B. slid the back of the box into place again.

D. B. nodded. "Plenty of airholes," she said. "Oz and I checked."

They crossed to the laundry room, and D. B. climbed into another cart. "Keep your fingers crossed, Agent Henshaw," she said, as Nigel covered her with fresh towels. "Let's just hope Oz's plan works."

CHAPTER 29

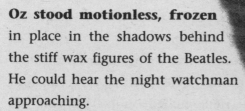

DAY TWO
DECEMBER 24
2100 HOURS

Oz stood motionless, frozen in place in the shadows behind the stiff wax figures of the Beatles. He could hear the night watchman approaching.

"Oi, old-timer!" the guard called out, his flashlight darting this way and that among the museum's wax inhabitants.

Oz held his breath. Getting inside Madame Tussaud's had been easier than he'd expected. Squeak was right—the night watchman had fallen for his story hook, line, and sinker.

"Lost your specs, did you? On Christmas Eve? We can't have that, can we," he'd chuckled kindly, ushering Oz inside. "Bet you'll be wanting them for tomorrow morning, to see the grandkiddies open their presents."

Oz had nodded at this, trying to look both pathetic and grateful, and as the night watchman headed for the lost and found, he'd simply tiptoed off in the other direction toward the exhibits.

"Where'd he get to, then?" the night watchman grumbled, drawing closer. "Old fool."

Sweat broke out on Oz's forehead as the night watchman drew closer. He couldn't be discovered—he just couldn't! Not when he was this close to his goal. He held his breath, squatting down beside the seated figure of the group's drummer. *John, Paul, George, Ringo—and Lardo,* Oz thought ruefully, hoping the man wouldn't notice an extra, somewhat tubby Beatle.

He was in luck. The night watchman's eyes slid right over the display as he passed by, and he disappeared down the hall still muttering to himself.

Oz waited what he hoped was enough time for the man to be safely out of hearing range, then tiptoed out from behind the drum set. He switched on his penlight. All around, wax faces stared at him in the darkness. Through his blurred gaze, they appeared alarmingly lifelike, and it seemed to Oz as he lurched out from behind the Beatles that they followed his every movement with their sightless glass eyes.

Oz's pulse began to race. This place was giving him the creeps. Perspiration dripped down his nose. He reached up automatically to prod his glasses into place, then stopped. He wasn't wearing his glasses.

As he searched frantically for Winston Churchill, he passed presidents and princes, politicians and princesses, the famous and the infamous alike. Charlie Chaplin. Marilyn Monroe. Gandhi. Rock stars galore. Athletes and actors—even James Bond! Well, a movie star who played Agent 007. Oz skirted the Chamber of Horrors—at least he didn't have to go

down there looking for the prime minister—and two minutes later, after twelve more heart-stopping inspections of frozen figures, including the queen, he found Winston Churchill.

Oz regarded him for a moment. The great statesman was a barrel of a man, and his genial bulldog face was set in lines of courage and strength.

"Sorry, sir," he whispered, clenching the penlight between his teeth and patting the prime minister down. His fingers searched the smooth, silken material of his waistcoat for something—anything—that might be the Summoner. But there was nothing.

Oz frowned. Had Sir Edmund been misinformed? Maybe it was sewn inside a different waistcoat, one packed away in a trunk in an attic somewhere. Sweating heavily now, Oz worked his way over every inch of the waistcoat again. Still nothing.

"It's not here!" he whispered aloud. Churchill didn't reply, but it seemed to Oz that the wax figure regarded him with sympathy. What was he going to do? The mice were counting on him. London was counting on him. Thousands and thousands of lives could depend on the outcome of his part of the mission. He couldn't give up yet. He wouldn't. He started up at the top of the waistcoat for the third time.

"Aha!" he cried softly. There it was: a narrow, almost undetectable bump inside the very bottom of the front left hem. "Gotcha!"

Oz clicked open Squeak's mini-penknife and began to slice at the material. No careful picking of the hem; there wasn't time. The fabric, worn with age, split open almost of its own accord. Something bright flashed in the beam of Oz's tiny flashlight, and as it started to tumble toward the ground he caught it in his hand. He held it close to the light. The Summoner!

Oz inspected it curiously. It looked like a dog whistle. A very unusual and beautiful dog whistle. The slender silver tube was etched with a pattern of what looked like *v*'s. Birds from what Squeak had told him. The swallows of the Secret Air Service who would respond to the call. If they still remembered it, that is. Oz pocketed the Summoner, along with the penknife, and smoothed Winston Churchill as best he could.

"Thank you, sir," he said, bowing to the wax figure. "It was an honor meeting you."

Trying hard not to bump into anything—or anyone—Oz began to tiptoe his way toward the exit. As he neared the door, he heard footsteps approaching again. The night watchman! Panicking, Oz ran for the door and pushed it open, setting off a high-pitched alarm.

"Oi!" cried the guard.

No time for pretending to be an old man now. Oz started to run. He pounded blindly down the sidewalk, pushing past pedestrians right and left. "Excuse me! Pardon me! Coming through!" he called.

He ran until he could run no more, then stopped and leaned over, panting. He glanced behind him, fully expecting to see the museum's night watchman.

But he wasn't there. No one was pursuing him. The

man must have given up. Oz stood up and squinted at his surroundings, still wheezing. Where was he?

After a few false starts and a lot of assistance from several passersby, Oz stumbled his way to Baker Street station. He carefully followed the directions that Squeak had given him, and he soon arrived, breathless, at St. Paul's Cathedral.

Oz checked his watch. He was running behind schedule. It was already past time for intermission at the concert. D. B. and Nigel must be frantic with worry! He trotted up the marble steps. Squeak had told him he'd have no problem getting in. The humans always held a Christmas Eve service at St. Paul's that was open to the public, she'd said. Sure enough, as he approached the huge carved door, Oz heard music inside. He pushed it open and stepped inside.

Oz stopped in his tracks. He gazed around in wonder. The cathedral's soaring stone interior was lit with the glow of a thousand candles, maybe more. Directly in front of him was a life-size manger scene. Most beautiful of all, however, was the music. It came from the far end of the great church, where a choir of boys lofted carols heavenward toward the arched dome.

Oz shook himself. *Get a grip, Levinson—you've got a job to do.* Skirting the manger, he found his way to the staircase leading to the Whispering Gallery. Beyond that, up at the top of the dome, lay his destination: the Stone Gallery.

"Sorry, mate, can't go up there. It's closed for the evening," said a warden, barring the door.

Oz gulped. He checked his watch again. It was nearly nine

thirty! Only a half hour left until Rodent Rooter's deadline. If he didn't reach the Stone Gallery soon and contact the S.A.S., there would be no way to rescue Glory and the orphans and nab Goldwhiskers's credit card. There'd be no way to cancel the exterminations. Operation S.M.A.S.H. would hurtle forward, and the mice of London would be doomed.

What would James Bond do? Oz asked himself. *Be your character,* came the reply. *Act the part.* Oz cupped his hand behind his ear. "Eh?" he said.

"I SAID IT'S CLOSED FOR THE EVENING!" repeated the warden, speaking into his ear slowly and loudly.

Oz slumped sadly. "Pity," he croaked. "I've come all the way from America to see it." This was partly true; he *had* come all the way from America.

The warden sighed. "Well, I suppose I can make an exception for an older gent like yourself. It's those noisy kids we need to keep out."

He held the door open and ushered Oz inside. "Lovely view of the manger from up there," he noted. "Watch yourself, though. Two hundred and fifty-nine steps to the top. Sure you're up to it, old-timer?"

Oz nodded. "Stronger than I look," he creaked, which was true.

He started to climb. And climb. And climb. Up and up and up the stone steps led, winding their way through the cathedral's thick walls. Oz glanced anxiously at his watch and climbed a little faster. His shirt was soaked with sweat. He reached the Whispering Gallery—a narrow stone balcony that circled the interior of the great dome—and paused for a second to catch his breath. Oz had no idea if the view of the manger was lovely or not. He couldn't see a thing, just the blur of light from the candles. Nor did he have any idea if a whisper would truly carry across the dome to the other side, as he was all by himself. It was just him and the candlelight and that achingly beautiful music, carols as old as time and as familiar as his own name.

Oz skirted the balcony to the door that led farther upward to the Stone Gallery. It was unlocked. Good. He pushed it open and began to climb again. On and on and on he climbed, until there was hardly a breath left in his body. Finally, gasping, knees buckling beneath him, he stumbled out onto the balcony—an exterior one this time— that offered visitors a spectacular view of the city.

Oz reached into his pocket and pulled out the slip of paper with the coordinates for the Secret Air Service, along with the Summoner. He held the silver whistle in his hand for a minute. Hidden in the lining of Winston Churchill's waistcoat since the end of World War II, it had not been blown for more than half a century. He was holding a piece of history.

Oz raised it to his lips and blew. No sound emerged. Nothing at all. Oz blew harder. Still the Summoner was silent. Was it blocked? He peered at it in concern. Or was it like a dog whistle, then, so highly pitched that the sound couldn't be picked up by the human ear? He blew again and again and again, pausing each time to search the night sky. Nothing.

Oz leaned back against the wall behind him, thoroughly disheartened. He'd come so far, and now this! It was nothing but a dead end. What would he tell Sir Edmund? What would happen to the mice of London? And what would happen to Glory? He'd failed them all. He'd even failed himself. Scotland Yard would arrest him and D. B. and his mother the minute tonight's concert was over. Oz closed his eyes and fought back tears.

CHAPTER 30

DAY TWO
DECEMBER 24
1635 HOURS

"Any word yet?" asked Bunsen,
glancing anxiously at the clock. It was past
nine-thirty in London. Exactly twenty-five
minutes left until Rodent Rooter's deadline.
Less than half an hour left to foil Operation
S.M.A.S.H.

Julius shook his head in regret. "Afraid not, Mr. Burner."

The lab mouse was visibly shaken. The Video Scrambler was
still down, and although Sir Edmund had been true to his word,
providing frequent updates via e-mail, it wasn't the same as
hearing the latest reports directly from him. The uncertainty
was getting to Bunsen. He could hardly bear the thought of his
sweetheart trapped in the clutches of not just Roquefort
Dupont, but Stilton Piccadilly and this evil Goldwhiskers, as
well. There'd been no news yet from Squeak, either. Had she
been able to intercept Oz and the S.A.S.? Was the rescue mission
underway? The tension was taking its toll on the lab mouse.

"Is there still hope of rescue?" he asked.

"There's always hope," said Julius calmly. "Morning

Glory Goldenleaf and Bubble Westminster are both highly trained, elite members of the finest espionage agencies in the world. And don't forget, Glory's been in tight spots before and has come through with flying colors."

Bunsen did not find this reassuring. "That stupid riddle!" he moaned, wringing his pale paws. "Why didn't I run it through A.M.I.? I can't believe the troops and the S.A.S. were sent to the wrong place!"

"No point kicking ourselves," soothed Julius. "The Royal Guard and the Welsh Rarebit Regiment are being moved out even as we speak. They may still arrive at the London Eye in time."

"But what if they don't?" cried Bunsen.

"Then Sir Edmund will begin the evacuation."

"But Glory and the orphans!"

Julius eyed him soberly. "You know as well as I do that sometimes sacrifices must be made in this business."

Bunsen's milky coat grew even paler. "'The noblest motive is the public good,'" he whispered. The Spy Mice Agency's motto.

Julius nodded sadly.

"Is evacuation even possible?" asked Bunsen.

The elder mouse hesitated. "I'm sure they'll be able to save a portion of the population," he replied finally.

Bunsen began to pace back and forth. "They have to get there in time! They just have to!"

Julius checked his watch surreptitiously. No point in alarming his colleague any further. He was already wound up far too tightly. But Bunsen was right. Time was fast running out—and with it, all hope of rescue.

CHAPTER 31

DAY TWO
DECEMBER 24
2135 HOURS

"Sparklies? Check!" said **Gold**-whiskers, peering into the velvet pouch he clutched in his manicured paws. "Credit card?" He whipped the gold plastic rectangle out from where he'd stashed it behind his left ear. "Check!" Into the bag it went. "Koh-i-Noor?" The big rat stood up and turned around, examining the place where his enormous gray bottom had just been. He'd been squatting protectively on the large gem, like a furry hen trying to hatch an extremely valuable egg. He glanced suspiciously over at the other two rats nearby. "Check!" he said, and whisked the Koh-i-Noor in with his other treasures.

"Somehow, watching a rat pack—or is that 'pack rat'?—isn't how I imagined spending Christmas Eve in London," Glory whispered to Bubble.

"I know what you mean," Bubble whispered back.

They were all—rats, spy mice, orphans—crammed into a plastic pet carrier. The mice were at one end; the rats at the other. With everything in place for tomorrow morning's attack, and the Koh-i-Noor in his possession at last, Goldwhiskers was preparing to skip town. "The south of France," Glory had overheard him tell Dupont and Piccadilly. "I've had my banker wire the funds ahead. I've always fancied a villa on the Riviera."

First, however, he was determined to deal with the orphans—and his two captive spy mice.

The night wind whistled through the airholes in the pet carrier, and Glory shivered. A courier had picked them up from outside Goldwhiskers's office more than an hour ago. After consulting the directions in the envelope taped to the handle—"'Surprise Christmas present!'" the man had read aloud. "'Do not open! Deliver to Jubilee Gardens!'"—he'd toted the carrier downstairs and slung it into the back of the waiting limousine. Glory and the others had remained there in the dark, bumping along through London's busy streets, until they'd reached their destination. Once at Jubilee Gardens, the limousine driver had dutifully deposited them by the gate and driven off.

Glory's paws were bound behind her with string, as were Bubble's. The orphans huddled around them, their eyes bright with fear.

"Please, miss, do you know where Master's taking us?" one of them ventured in a shaky whisper.

"What's your name, little one?" Glory whispered back.

"Twist."

"Please to meet you, Twist. I'm Glory. I wish I could answer your question, but I have no idea." She gazed at the rest of the orphans. "You must be brave, though, all of you. And try not to worry," she added stoutly. "We'll find a way out of this mess."

Glory spoke with a confidence she didn't feel. She'd never been so scared in all her life. Not even in Dupont's lair; not even when she'd been trapped on that balloon with a whole galaxy of the world's worst rat kingpins, including a pair of ferocious mousivores. No, this was far, far worse. Because what she was feeling this time wasn't so much fear for herself— although that was certainly a factor. It was fear for the mouse- lings. Glory was terrified for them. She couldn't bear the thought of all those young lives being cut tragically short. She wanted desperately to rescue them from the cruel fate that Goldwhiskers had in store, but now she feared she wouldn't be able to. Time was running out. Fast.

Glory glanced over at the trio of rats, who were hunched together at the opposite end of the pet carrier, arguing.

"I say we skip the drama and just shove the whole thing into the river," snarled Roquefort Dupont. "Or feed them to the wharf cats." He licked his thin rat lips. "We could take turns. That would be fun."

"This isn't about *fun*!" roared Goldwhiskers. "It's about *revenge*." A streetlight overhead cast thin shards of light through the sprinkling of holes on top of the pet carrier, and Glory caught a lunatic glint in the big rat's eyes. Goldwhiskers had definitely gone round the bend.

"Really?" replied Stilton Piccadilly. "So deep down, it's

still just claws and jaws for you after all. You can take the rat out of the sewer, but you can't take the sewer out of the rat. Eh, Double G?"

Goldwhiskers turned on him. "Stop calling me that!" he snarled. He nodded at the Sovereign's Ring, which hung from a piece of string around Dupont's mangy neck. "You two have been paid. You've got the ring; you've got your exterminators. There's nothing keeping you here. I can take care of the mice myself."

Dupont slunk across the carrier and jabbed Glory with his ugly snout. "I'm not so sure about that," he growled. "Especially this one. She's sly. Think I'd better stick around and make sure the job's done right."

"Suit yourself," said Goldwhiskers. "Let's get on with it. You two take the spies, I'll manage the mouselings."

Dupont snapped his fangs, and Glory rose shakily to her hind paws. Beside her, Bubble did the same. As Goldwhiskers advanced toward them, the orphans crowded closer to the older mice. Twist clung to Glory's tail; Farthing climbed onto her back and wound his paws tightly around her neck. Dodge crouched behind Bubble.

"Come to Master," coaxed Goldwhiskers. He pried Farthing off Glory and gave Twist a sharp kick. The mouseling cried out in pain. "You never would have amounted to anything, anyway," scoffed the big rat. "I lied. You're nothing but a useless street urchin." He turned to Dodge. *"Et tu,* Dodge?" he said, reaching out with a paw and extracting her from behind Bubble. He pressed his snout close to her tiny nose. She shrank back, and he gave a snort of disgust. "And to think that I trusted you."

The big rat cracked his hairless tail like a whip. The orphans flinched. Goldwhiskers looked over at Glory and grinned. "What is it you Yanks say? Head 'em up and move 'em out?"

Glory glared back at him defiantly. "Only one problem, cowboy."

"What's that?"

"You're all hat and no cattle. Or maybe I should say all *rat* and no cattle."

Goldwhiskers eyes glowed red with rage. "Shut her up, would you?"

"Gladly," said Dupont, and clamped a large, flea-bitten, herring-scented paw over Glory's mouth.

Goldwhiskers pried open the door of the pet carrier and herded them all outside. Dupont slung Glory over his back. From her upside-down vantage point, she watched, helpless, as Stilton Piccadilly picked up Bubble by the scruff of his neck with his fangs. Then Dupont bounced forward, and for one brief second Glory found herself eye to eye with Fumble. She thought she caught a glimpse of something in his expression—pity, perhaps, or possibly just fear. No one was safe tonight from the fury of the rats. Not even a slave.

Once outside, Glory looked up and gasped. Towering above them stood the London Eye, the huge observation wheel on the bank of the river Thames. It was lit up like a

Christmas tree, its football-shaped glass capsules circling slowly through the air.

"Up we go!" said Goldwhiskers. He nudged the orphans onto a nearby concrete footing, then herded them onto one of the massive steel cables that anchored the wheel to the Waterloo Millennium Pier.

Beneath her, Glory felt Roquefort Dupont inch his way up the cable, his sharp claws rasping on the cold steel. Behind them followed Stilton Piccadilly, still carrying Bubble Westminster. When Goldwhiskers reached the top, he paused until the other two rats caught up.

"On my signal," he said.

He waited until one of the oval capsules was directly underneath them, then brushed the mouselings forward with a sweep of his tail. They tumbled through the air, ears over tails, landing atop the capsule with a patter of tiny thuds. Goldwhiskers leaped aboard behind them, quickly followed by Dupont and Piccadilly, who dumped Glory and Bubble in a heap and stood over them, glaring.

"Now we'll see who's Master!" cried Goldwhiskers. "Try and foil my plans, will you? Disobey my orders, will you? Say your good-byes to London, mouselings! When we reach the top, it's curtains for you!"

Glory worked frantically at the string that bound her paws together. She had to do something! She peered through the glass beneath her. No one was inside the capsule. In fact, no one was inside any of the capsules. It was long past closing time and the London Eye was eerily empty, spinning silently through one last maintenance cycle. On the ground far below, Glory could see the cleaning crew. They swarmed aboard as each capsule docked, sweeping and polishing and shining the glass and steel enclosures. Glory couldn't get their attention even if she tried.

No, she and Bubble were on their own. Glory looked over at her colleague, who was working just as determinedly at his own bonds. Next to him slumped Fumble, still reeking of herring. Around his neck was the frayed leash that tethered him to Roquefort Dupont's hind paw.

As the great wheel moved slowly, majestically skyward, carrying the mice to their fate, Glory gazed at the city spreading out beneath them in all its ancient glory. *I guess I'm finally getting my tour of London,* she thought morosely. She looked upriver toward Big Ben. Nearly quarter to ten. Time was running out for her, that was certain. Somewhere in the darkness out there was MICE-6 headquarters. She wondered if her colleagues had been able to decipher Goldwhiskers's riddle—surely a rescue team would have been here by now if they had! She glanced downriver toward the Savoy and the city's other huge clock face, the one that marked Goldwhiskers's lair at 80 Strand, then back toward the ornate Houses of Parliament, behind which rose the stately spires of Westminster Abbey. Not a pigeon in sight. Glory's sense of doom deepened. There was no hope of rescue then. Not this time.

And what about the rest of London's mice? Would Sir

Edmund and the others be able to stop Operation S.M.A.S.H.? Had they even received her frantic warning? If not—well, she wouldn't be the only one who was doomed. Sadly, Glory stared off into the distance toward the illuminated facade of Buckingham Palace. The Prince of Tails was going to be very disappointed in her. In all of them.

As the observation car rose closer to its zenith, Goldwhiskers began herding the orphans closer to the capsule's curved edge. The mouselings looked down at the river far, far below and shrieked in terror.

"Those two as well!" the big rat ordered, and Dupont and Piccadilly began to force Glory and Bubble toward the orphans.

Never give in, thought Glory bravely. *Never, never, never, never. I won't go to my death in fear.* No way was she going to allow Goldwhiskers—and especially not Roquefort Dupont—the satisfaction of seeing her afraid. She reminded herself of the generations of noble mice who had put their lives on the line before her as they faced down the forces of evil. *Lux tenebras exstinguit,* she thought. *Light extinguishes darkness. Hold your candle high, Glory Goldenleaf,* she told herself, and bravely prepared to die.

CHAPTER 32

DAY TWO
DECEMBER 24
2140 HOURS

Oz heard them before he saw them. A soft rustling filled the air at first, like leaves snatched up in a puff of wind. He opened his eyes and grabbed the railing that encircled the balcony. The stone was cold beneath his hands.

The sound drew closer, and louder: the whispery flapping of many wings. Hope soared in Oz, and he craned his neck, smiling in anticipation as he tried to spot the rescue birds. The S.A.S. had heard his call! The Summoner still worked after all these years!

He squinted at the flock of dark forms that suddenly materialized, silhouetted against the full moon. As they drew close enough for him to make them out more clearly, his smile faded. Oz drew back against the cathedral wall with a gasp.

The Summoner had worked, all right. But Squeak was wrong. The S.A.S. wasn't a squadron of swallows. The Summoner had not brought birds. It had brought bats. Thousands and thousands of bats.

Oz swallowed hard. He was shaking uncontrollably. "The name is Levinson. Oz Levinson," he whispered aloud, trying not to hear the soft, leathery flapping of their wings. He had to go through with this if he wanted to save Glory. He held the Summoner aloft and managed to croak out the code signal, just as Squeak had taught him: *"Lux tenebras exstinguit!"*

The wind snatched away his words, and for a moment there was no response. Then he felt something brush against his face. He choked back a scream.

"What issssss it?" he heard, or thought he heard. The voice was soft and sibilant, nearly as soft as the bats' own silent wings. "Issssss not moussssse."

"Issssss human," came another voice, soft as a sigh. "Not to be trusssssssted."

Oz squeezed his eyes tightly shut. He couldn't look. He just couldn't. *James Bond would look,* he told himself. Agent 007 laughed in the face of danger. Oz cracked one eye open. He found himself face-to-furry-face with an upside-down bat. He quickly shut the eye again. Laugh? He felt more like crying. Every nerve in his body was screaming, *run!* But Oz thought again of Glory, and the orphans, and all the other mice in London who were depending on him. He stood his ground.

"He knowssssss the sssssignal," whispered a third voice.

"No," said the second voice. "Imposssssster. Not to be trusssssted."

"Wait!" called Oz in desperation, as he heard the bats

begin to fly away. Mustering every ounce of courage he possessed, he opened both eyes and took a step forward. The bats hesitated, dipping and fluttering before him like dark moths against the moonlit sky. "The name is Levinson," Oz announced firmly. "Oz Levinson. Friend of mice and fellow soldier against evil. Against rats." *And sharks,* he almost added. He paused, unsure of what else he should say.

A single bat detached itself from the flock and circled closer. He stared at Oz with fathomless, unblinking eyes. "Fellow sssssoldier against ratssssss?" he whispered, his voice a low hiss.

Oz nodded.

"Batsssss hate ratsssss."

Oz nodded encouragingly. "That's right. And the mice are in trouble tonight. Just as they were a very long time ago. During the Blitz. The rats are holding some of them prisoner right now. Mouselings. They're planning to kill them, and to exterminate the rest of London. We need your help."

"Moussssssselings?"

Oz nodded.

"Exxxxxxterminate?"

"Yes," said Oz soberly.

"We haven't heard the sssssssummons in a very long time," sighed the bat.

"No," agreed Oz. "Not since Sir Peregrine Inkwell."

"You knew Sssssssssir Peregrine?"

Oz shook his head. "I'm here under orders from his

great-grandson, Sir Edmund Hazelnut-Cadbury. He's the head of MICE-Six now."

The bat flitted away again and rejoined the others. Oz could hear them consulting amongst themselves as they flickered in the air above him, their words like the whisper of dried leaves.

The three who had spoken detached themselves from the others and darted toward him again with such speed that he drew back in alarm. They swooped to a stop at eye level and clung by their claws, upside down, to the stone parapet overhead. The bats' small, eerie faces were hideous and wild, their mouths bristling with sharp, evil-looking fangs. Oz gulped. *How do I get myself into these things?* he wondered.

"What are our orderssssssss?" whispered the leader.

"It's a r-r-r-escue mission," stuttered Oz. "Glory's been captured."

"Who issssss Glory?" the bat asked.

"Glory Goldenleaf. She's a spy mouse," Oz explained. "A very brave spy mouse, and one of my best friends in the whole world. She's been captured with one of her colleagues, Bubble Westminster, and a whole bunch of orphan mouselings. They need to be airlifted to safety."

He reached into his pocket for the slip of paper with the coordinates to the Savoy Hotel and read them off. Then he held up the paper, trying not to flinch as a leathery wing brushed the back of his hand when one of the bats snatched it from him.

The three bats studied the note, then looked back at him and nodded their fierce little heads. "Yesssssss," they whispered in unison. And without another word they rose into the air above St. Paul's Cathedral and disappeared into the night.

CHAPTER 33

DAY TWO
DECEMBER 24
2145 HOURS

"Be brave, mouselings," Glory whispered, as Big Ben chimed the quarter hour. The orphans clustered closely around her. Twist was glued to her side, and Farthing had clambered up onto her back again. He was sucking his tail furiously. At her side, Bubble Westminster stood his ground staunchly.

"It's been an honor working with you, Glory," Bubble said.

"Likewise, Bubble. You're true-blue."

Standing shoulder to shoulder, the two spy mice agents faced the waiting rats. Several more minutes ticked by. Finally, the London Eye reached the height of its arc. As it did, it seemed to pause and hang there in space. The rats closed in. For each step forward that Goldwhiskers, Dupont, and Piccadilly took, the two spy mice and the throng of mouselings took one step back, until they teetered at the very brink of the glass observation car's sloping edge. Glory drew a deep breath, still determined to meet her end with the dignity befitting both a Goldenleaf and a member of the Spy Mice Agency.

"Are you really going to go through with it, Goldwhiskers?" she said. "Send all these innocent mouselings to their deaths?"

"Nobody double-crosses Double G," snarled Goldwhiskers, who had completely reverted to his sewer-bred roots. "Especially not mouselings!"

"They should call you Coldwhiskers," said Glory bitterly. "You've got nothing but an ice cube for a heart."

The big rat sneered and closed in. The tiny flame of hope that Glory had been tending inside sputtered and went out. It was too late for rescue. She was out of time.

Then Glory caught a flutter of something in the distance, over Goldwhiskers's shoulder. There it was again! A shadow flitting across the face of Big Ben. Probably nothing. But she decided to stall for time, just in case.

"Isn't it tradition for condemned prisoners to be granted a last request?" she asked.

Goldwhiskers's eyes narrowed. "Be quick about it, then," he said.

"I'd love to see the Koh-i-Noor one more time," Glory replied.

Goldwhiskers regarded her shrewdly. "This better not be a trick."

Glory turned around to show that her paws were still bound. The big rat gave a curt nod and opened his velvet duffel bag. He reached in and drew out the gem. If possible, the diamond was even more dazzling in the moonlight. The moon's silver rays twinkled and danced across its luminous facets like starry lights on a Christmas tree. Mice and rats alike fell silent for a moment under the Koh-i-Noor's spell.

And then—

"INCOMING!" screamed Roquefort Dupont, as thousands of bats dropped from the night sky. Leading them, astride her pigeon, was Squeak Savoy.

Instantly, all was chaos. The mouselings shrieked and scattered, even more terrified of the ferocious-looking bats than they were of their rat captors. They tumbled across the top of the glass observation car like furry marbles, and Goldwhiskers scrambled after them, furiously trying to round them up. Dupont and Piccadilly swatted frantically at the dive-bombing bats, who nipped at the rats' heads and snouts like moths around a trio of flames.

Glory and Bubble instantly moved into back-to-back position, the emergency maneuver they'd learned in spy school, and untied each other's paws.

"Get the credit card!" cried Squeak, glancing anxiously at Big Ben. "Code Red!"

Her urgent words fueled her two colleagues to ever greater efforts, and the moment they were free, Glory and Bubble raced toward Goldwhiskers. He saw them coming and slashed at them with an enormous paw, sending them spinning away, tail over whiskers. Glory rolled to a stop right in front of Roquefort Dupont.

"How convenient," he said, and dove for her, dragging Fumble, who was still attached to his hind paw, with him. Glory rolled quickly to one side. Dupont missed her by a whisker. He lunged again. Glory rolled back the other way, but Dupont was too quick for her this time. He pounced, grabbing her with his sharp claws, and bared his yellow teeth in a hideous smile of triumph.

The smile quickly turned to a snarl of terror, however, as behind him Fumble stood up. Glory's former colleague teetered on the edge of the observation car, shot Glory a cryptic glance, and slowly toppled over the side.

Glory gasped.

"NO!" screeched Dupont, as the leash slithered after Fumble, dragging him with it. He let go of Glory and scrabbled for a pawhold, but Fumble's weight was enough to tow him slowly, agonizingly, bit by bit, toward the edge. The rat's sharp claws scraped and clawed across the glass as he slid, emitting a hideous screech, like fingernails dragging across a chalkboard.

Stilton Piccadilly saw him and rushed across the glass, swatting bats fiercely out of his way.

"Grab my paw, Piccadilly!" screamed Dupont.

Instead, the head of London's rat forces reached out and yanked the Sovereign's Ring from around his rival's scruffy neck. "I think I'll grab this instead."

"DOUBLE-CROSSER!" howled Roquefort Dupont, his final words echoing as he vanished over the side.

Glory lay there for a moment in shock. What had just

happened? Had Fumble slipped, or had he sacrificed himself in a bid to save her and the orphans?

"Glory, I need that credit card *NOW*!" Squeak cried desperately.

All of her Silver Skateboard training kicked in as Glory responded to her colleague's urgent plea. No time to think about Fumble—she had to act. She scrambled up and raced toward Goldwhiskers.

Across from her, Bubble was bravely battling Stilton Piccadilly. Overhead, Glory saw members of the S.A.S. plucking terrified orphans off the observation car one by one, while Goldwhiskers, who appeared to have come completely unhinged, swung at them with his gem-filled velvet pouch.

"Those are MY mice!" he thundered. "MASTER'S mouselings!" There was a loud *THWACK* as the pouch connected to a bat. Stunned, the creature dropped like a stone. Goldwhiskers whirled the pouch around his head and prepared to deliver the final blow.

Glory dove for him. "No you don't, Goldwhiskers," she cried, crunching down on his tail with her sharp little teeth.

The big rat yelped and swung around with a murderous glance. Before he could attack, however, a whole squadron of bats surrounded him. Grabbing him by his ears, whiskers, paws, and tail, they lifted him bodily into the air. He dangled there, howling in frustration.

"I'll take that," said Glory, plucking the velvet pouch from his grasp. "Diamonds are a mouse's best friend, remember?" She rummaged through the pouch's contents. "And credit cards aren't bad, either. Here, Squeak!" she called, holding up the card.

Squeak swooped from the sky and grabbed it. She pressed the button on her transmitter and crisply called out the numbers on the back to MICE-6.

"Well done!" Glory heard Sir Edmund say. "Well done, indeed!"

Bubble appeared, panting. "What was that all about?" he asked.

Squeak tapped the credit card's security code with her paw. "Couldn't cancel the exterminations without this," she explained. "Bunsen figured it out. Problem was, we only had until ten o'clock to do it."

Glory turned and stared at Big Ben. The fur on the back of her neck prickled as she saw that the clock's hands pointed to one minutes til ten. "We almost didn't make it," she whispered.

"A very close call," agreed Bubble soberly.

"Indeed," said Squeak. "But we did make it, thanks to you two." She slipped the credit card into her backpack. "I'd better take this to HQ. The Royal Guard is waiting for you below."

And with that she flew off.

Suddenly, Roquefort Dupont reappeared over the side of the sloping glass observation-car roof. Glory and Bubble clutched each other in fright, then relaxed when they saw that he, too, was dangling safely from S.A.S. claws.

There was no sign of Fumble, however.

"Let me go! You don't know who you're dealing with!" screamed Dupont, struggling with all his considerable might. "I am Roquefort Dupont! The great-great-great-great-great-great-great-great-great-great-great-great-great-great-grandson of Camembert Dupont!"

One of the bats hovered in front of Dupont's ugly snout. "You are the great-great-great-great-great-great-great-great-great-great-great-great-great-great-grandssssssson of Camembert Dupont?" he repeated.

"Heard of me, have you?" sneered Dupont. "That's right, buddy, and you and your batbrained friends here better not forget it! Release me now, and I'll go easy on you."

"Releassssse you?" whispered the bat. "I think not. We have an old, old sssssscore to sssssettle. Cccccenturies old." He flew over to Glory and Bubble. "Permisssssssion to disssssspose of the prissssssoner."

"Granted," Glory replied promptly.

"Take them both," offered Bubble, gesturing toward Stilton Piccadilly. "Two for one, just for tonight. Christmas Eve special."

"We'll keep this, though," added Glory, plucking the Sovereign's Ring out of Piccadilly's paws. She tucked it inside the velvet pouch, then nodded at Goldwhiskers. "And that one as well, for now."

The bat inclined his ugly head and flapped away. He signaled to the rest of the S.A.S., and in a trice Roquefort Dupont and Stilton Piccadilly were ferried off, still thrashing and snarling in protest. The last that Glory saw of them was their silhouetted forms soaring across the illuminated face of Big Ben as the great bell rang out its famous chime. *BONG! BONG! BONG!* tolled the bell, a total of ten times to mark the hour. The sound came as music to Glory's ears. What had almost been a death toll for her—and for the mice of London—was now the sweet sound of victory.

"That's that, then," said Bubble, watching as one of the bats finally managed to corner the nimble Farthing. The mouseling squealed, puddled, then went limp as the S.A.S. member gripped him firmly and flew off toward Nibbleswick.

"Not quite," said Glory, pointing to the still-struggling Goldwhiskers. "One last Christmas Eve crisis to deal with."

She and Bubble drew closer to the big rat.

"Looks like they were right about the curse of the Koh-i-Noor," she told him, patting the velvet pouch. "It certainly proved unlucky for you."

"That's MY diamond!" Goldwhiskers howled, bucking and snarling in fury. His efforts to free himself were in vain, however. The bats had him in a ferociously tight grip.

"Not anymore," said Glory, handing the pouch to Bubble. "Would you mind carrying these? We'll get the Royal Guard to take us back to 80 Strand. I have plans for our boogeyrat here."

CHAPTER 34

DAY TWO
DECEMBER 24
2225 HOURS

Oz glanced nervously at his watch, then across the row of red velvet seats. He, D. B., Nigel, and his father were seated together in the front row, flanked by police. Standing in the stage wings and at every entrance were more policemen, as well as detectives from Scotland Yard. No one was taking any more chances tonight. Not after Oz had been caught reentering the opera house. Dressed in a disguise, no less.

"Where's Priscilla?" whispered his father.

"Napping," Oz whispered back, which was true.

There had been no word yet from Glory or any of the other spy mice. Oz had no clue what was going on in the skies over London. He didn't know if Operation S.M.A.S.H. had been foiled, or whether the S.A.S. had rescued his friends and retrieved the Crown Jewels. He glanced at his watch again. It was nearly ten thirty. The finale was about to start. Surely he should have heard something by now.

"Stop fidgeting!" scolded D. B. "You too, Nigel!"

Nigel stared at the stage. "Do you think it's really going to work?"

"Of course," said D. B. confidently. "Our plans always work."

"Well, mostly," added Oz.

Mr. Henshaw raised his baton, and the orchestra struck the opening chords of "White Christmas." Oz, D. B., and Nigel sat up expectantly. Right on cue, fog began drifting across the stage.

"Dry ice," whispered D. B. "Just like you said, Oz."

Glittering paper snowflakes began drifting down from above the stage, and then, as if by magic, two enormous presents, one wrapped in red foil, one in silver, rose up through the floor. The audience gasped in wonder and began to applaud vigorously.

Beside him, the policeman shifted in his seat, and Oz looked over to see a detective from Scotland Yard coming down the aisle. He was frowning. He handed a note to the policeman next to Oz's father. A curtain fluttered up above in the Royal Box, and Oz saw a detective hand the queen a note as well. She frowned, and Oz's heart sank. This was it, then. The end of the line. He was going to be arrested.

The policeman read the note, then passed it to Luigi Levinson. Oz's father read it and let out a loud whoosh of relief. He leaned over and gave his son a bear hug. "Looks like we're off the hook!" he whispered. "They just found the jewels."

Oz glanced up at the Royal Box. The Queen smiled and

gave him a discreet nod. Oz, who hadn't realized he'd been holding his breath, exhaled. He smiled back. Everything was going to be okay! The S.A.S. had come through. Glory could fill him in on the details later.

Onstage, the two sopranos took their seats on the fake presents and began to sing. "I'm dreaming of a white Christmas, with every Christmas card I—whoops!" Prudence Winterbottom bounced slightly, and her voice shot up an octave. She quickly regained her composure and continued. "With every Christmas card I write!"

Suddenly, Prudence Winterbottom catapulted off the giant silver foil-wrapped present. With a loud thud, she landed flat on her backside on the stage floor. The orchestra wheezed to a halt. The top of the fake present flew off, and Priscilla Winterbottom, dressed as one of the *Nutcracker* ballet's giant rats, poked her furry gray costumed nose out. She sneezed.

Nigel Henshaw put his hand over his mouth and stifled a giggle.

"Slushbutt goes *down*!" whispered D. B. in triumph.

There was a moment of stunned silence from the audience. Priscilla climbed out of the box and stood there, blinking sleepily. She yawned, and peals of laughter rippled out across the Royal Opera House.

Her mother hauled herself upright. "Priscilla Winterbottom," she said in a furious stage whisper. "*What* do you think you're doing?"

Even the queen was laughing by now. Prudence

Winterbottom's ferret face flamed in humiliation. So did her daughter's.

Oz's father leaned over again. "You kids didn't have anything to do with this, did you?" he asked, his eyes twinkling.

Oz shrugged and gave him a rueful smile. He leaned over to D. B. and Nigel. "Looks like rats come in two-legged varieties as well as four," he whispered.

Priscilla scratched herself vigorously and sneezed. The audience roared again. Her mother grabbed her by one of her large, furry ears and dragged her offstage.

Lavinia Levinson looked out over the audience. Her gaze landed on Oz. She winked. "May your days be merry and bright!" she sang, her gorgeous soprano voice wafting up toward the ornate ceiling of the concert hall. "And may all your Christmases be white!"

CHAPTER 35

Back at 80 Strand, a pair of
detectives from Scotland Yard was
wrapping up the investigation at
the office of D. G. Whiskers, Esquire.

"Odd thing, don't you think?"
said one, crouching down and peering inside the plastic pet
carrier on the floor by the desk. The contents snarled at him
angrily.

"What?"

"This big rat here, with its whiskers painted gold."

The other detective looked up from his paperwork. He
shrugged. "Odd pet for an odd gent. Did you get a gawk at what
our Mr. Whiskers had stashed up in his attic?" He pointed to
the trapdoor in the ceiling and shook his head in disbelief. "All
that little dollhouse furniture? Definitely a nutter."

"I wonder where he's hiding?" said the first detective.

"Oh, we'll find him," said his colleague. "We always do.
Lucky for us one of his associates gave us a call and ratted
him out. He must have had to make a run for it, leaving his

pet behind like that. Not to mention the gems. He can't have gone far."

He swiveled around in the desk chair and patted the laptop computer that sat on the file cabinet behind him. "And there's this, too. The information in here will put D. G. Whiskers, Esquire, behind bars for life once we catch him. He can run, but he can't hide from Scotland Yard. Not after nicking the Crown Jewels."

The other detective was quiet for a while. Then he said, "You don't suppose . . ."

"I don't suppose what?"

The first man shrugged. "I dunno," he mumbled. "Foolish, I guess. But it's just such a coincidence. 'D. G. *Whiskers.*' The little furniture. Everything! You don't suppose this here rat with the golden whiskers had anything to do with it, do you?"

The other detective stared at him, speechless. "Do you mean to tell me you think that rat there stole the Crown Jewels? Next you'll be telling me you think the mice turned him in!"

His colleague gave him a sheepish smile. "Yeah, I suppose you're right. It's impossible. I guess it's just been a long day."

"Too long," said the other man, pushing back from the desk and packing up his briefcase. "Time to get you home." He picked up the pet carrier. Its contents growled softly. "We'll drop this by the Yard on the way, shall we? A little Christmas present for the lab. I'm sure they'll find a use for him—even if it's only as a holiday treat for the ferrets."

CHAPTER 36

Oz pulled the covers up under his chin and rolled over. He burrowed into his pillow and sighed a sigh of deep contentment. Suddenly, his eyes flew open. He sat bolt upright in bed. It was Christmas!

Throwing the covers back, he pulled on his bathrobe and slippers and trotted out into the hotel suite's fancy sitting room. No one else was awake yet but him. A beautiful little Christmas tree stood on the coffee table, twinkling with lights. Brightly wrapped presents were heaped around it, and he spent several happy minutes rifling through them, checking to see which ones were for him.

Also on the table was his mother's jewelery. Next to the neat pile of gems was a card that read, "Happy Christmas from your fans at Scotland Yard." Oz smiled. His mother would be thrilled.

The detectives had also returned his CD player and the grandpa shoes from the museum, he noted with relief. He'd been worried about how he was going to get Glory home again without them.

"Ahem," said a voice behind him. A very small voice.

Oz turned around. A dignified mouse stood at his feet. Beside him were Bubble, Squeak, and Glory.

"Merry Christmas, Oz!" said Glory.

The dignified mouse stepped forward. "Sir Edmund Hazelnut-Cadbury at your service," he said, extending his paw.

Oz crouched down and reached out a fingertip. Boy and mouse exchanged a gentle shake. "Pleased to meet you," said Oz.

"I never expected to find myself breaking the Mouse Code and speaking to a human," said Sir Edmund, gazing ruefully up at Oz. "But then again, my great-grandfather Peregrine Inkwell did, so it's not without precedent." He cleared his throat. "The mice of London owe you an enormous debt of gratitude, Ozymandias. We'd like to do something to thank you for your service to us."

"You already did," said Oz. "I thought I was going to spend the rest of my life in a dungeon for something I didn't do."

"True, the Koh-i-Noor and the Sovereign's Ring are safely back at the Tower of London where they belong," agreed Sir Edmund. "But nevertheless, without your efforts last night, Operation S. M. A. S. H. might not have been smashed to smithereens. The orphans might not have been rescued, and London might have been under attack even now. We at MICE-Six believe that heroism deserves to be recognized wherever possible." He held out his paw, and Squeak pulled something from her backpack and passed it to him. "And so, for exceptional bravery against the forces of evil, wherever found, this is for you, Ozymandias."

Sir Edmund held up a round object in both paws. Oz reached down and took it from him. It was a silver medallion about the size of dime. The words NEVER GIVE IN were stamped on one side, beneath a likeness of Winston Churchill. Oz flipped it over. On the other side was a picture of Sir Peregrine Inkwell, along with a single candle encircled by the words LUX TENEBRAS EXSTINGUIT. The MICE-6 crest.

"This was given to my great-grandfather by his hero and mine, Winston Churchill," said Sir Edmund. "They both would have been very proud of you, and I feel it's only fitting that you have it."

"Thank you," said Oz, stunned. He fingered the medallion. It reminded him of something he'd seen at the Spy Museum gift shop back in Washington. The hollow coins that spies used to conceal messages. Automatically, he pressed down on the edge of the medallion. It flew open. Sir Edmund gasped.

"I'm sorry!" cried Oz, glancing at him in alarm. "Did I do something wrong?"

"No, no, no," said Sir Edmund, flustered. "It's just that I didn't—I've never—bless my whiskers and tail! It never occurred to me that it might have a secret compartment."

"It's just like the coin I brought you from Washington!" said Glory.

Sir Edmund nodded. He craned his neck, clearly eager to see if there was anything inside. Oz placed the medallion on the floor and the mice clustered around it in excitement.

"Look!" said Sir Edmund, carefully removing a scrap of paper from the secret compartment. Oz watched as he unfolded it. "After all these years," the head of MICE-6 said softly.

At the top was a small pen-and-ink sketch of Churchill. His bulldog face bore a smile. On his shoulder perched Sir Peregrine Inkwell, saluting jauntily. The sketch was signed with the initials *W. C.*

"Churchill drew that," said Sir Edmund. "He was an accomplished artist, you know."

Beneath the sketch was a brief poem. Sir Edmund cleared his throat and read it aloud:

"'Side by side we stood, we two,
Through England's darkest hours.
We fought the foe with heads held high;
Now victory is ours.
In years to come, we hope these words
Bring comfort to our friends:
Stay straight on course and ne'er give in.
You'll triumph in the end.'"

The poem was signed with the initials *P. I.*

Sir Edmund sighed a deep, contented sigh. "A true poet, my great-grandfather. I shall live by these words always."

He folded up the scrap of paper reverently, then closed the medallion and passed it back to Oz. "Thank you, Ozymandias. For giving me a gift I could never have expected."

"You're welcome," Oz replied. He tucked Sir Edmund's present carefully into the pocket of his bathrobe. "Oh, and I have something for you." He pulled the Summoner out of the same pocket and passed it to the waiting mouse.

"Ah, so this is the famous Summoner," said the head of MICE-6, turning the intricately etched silver whistle over in his paws. "We'll put this in a safe place. Never know when it might be needed next." He cleared his throat. "I suppose we should discuss my new honorary agent."

"You mean Nigel?" said Oz sheepishly.

Sir Edmund nodded. "Julius believes that human children are an undervalued resource in our work. They travel under the radar, he says, and are excellent observers—particularly the quiet ones." He regarded Oz thoughtfully. "There's truth in that, I suppose. And if Nigel Henshaw proves half the young man that you are, I expect he'll make a fine addition to our team."

Oz breathed a sigh of relief. Sir Edmund wasn't mad at him!

The head of MICE-6 turned to Glory. "It appears Julius was right about you, too, Agent Goldenleaf," he told her. "You more than deserve that silver skateboard of yours. Like Ozymandias, you were an essential part of our mission last night, and we owe you, too, our everlasting gratitude. I look forward to working with you again in the future."

Glory's hopes soared. Did that mean she might be given a glamorous overseas posting?

"We must be off—Nibbleswick awaits," said Sir Edmund briskly.

"We've been invited to have breakfast with the orphans," Glory explained to Oz.

"Happy Christmas!" chorused Bubble and Squeak.

"Happy Christmas to you, too!" Oz replied, waving as his tiny friends filed out of the room.

CHAPTER 37

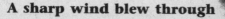

DAY THREE
DECEMBER 25
0730 HOURS

A sharp wind blew through St. James's Park, whirling twigs and leaves along the frozen ground like merry snowflakes. The park was deserted this cold Christmas morning, its many paths and walkways empty of humans. All across London, families and friends were gathering in the warmth of their homes to enjoy the holiday.

Deep in the twisted roots of an ancient oak tree, Glory, Bubble, Squeak, and Sir Edmund Hazelnut-Cadbury huddled together on the doorstep of the Nibbleswick Home for Little Wanderers, shivering. Sir Edmund raised the brass knocker (a brightly polished cuff link in the shape of a lion's head, foraged from the grounds of nearby Buckingham Palace) on the glossy red door and let it fall.

The door flew open, revealing a stout, efficient-looking house mouse. A crisp white apron was tied around her ample middle. "You'll be Sir Edmund, then," she said briskly. "We've been expecting you. Come along in out of the cold, all of you."

"Thank you, Matron," replied Sir Edmund.

Glory looked around the entrance hall. It was spotless, and it was furnished with practical items: a sturdy bench for mouselings to perch on while removing their backpacks from school; an umbrella holder (a foraged china toothpick caddy, again courtesy of Buckingham Palace); a long cabinet whose many pigeonholes displayed neat stacks of colorful mittens and hats for protecting small paws and ears from London's bitter winter wind. On one wall hung twin portraits of the orphanage's royal patrons, the Prince of Tails and the Duchess of Cornmeal. They looked very regal, thought Glory, in their coronets and red velvet capes.

"Fine set of ears, has our Prince of Tails," said Sir Edmund admiringly. "Very distinguished."

Glory nodded in agreement.

"Plays pigeon polo," added the elder mouse. "Quite well, in fact. And the duchess is a country mouse at heart, I hear—breeds crickets."

"The new arrivals are still sleeping," reported Matron. "It was all we could do to get a little cocoa in their tummies and wash them up last night, they were so wound up. Far too much excitement for such wee ones."

"Indeed," said Sir Edmund.

"May we see them?" asked Squeak.

"If you wish," said Matron. She directed them to a staircase next to the drawing room, where a fire crackled invitingly in the grate. "Breakfast will be ready shortly."

Leaving Sir Edmund warming himself by the fire, the

trio of spy mice tiptoed quietly upstairs to the orphanage's sleeping quarters.

Located in the tree's upper branches, the dormitory was a long, narrow room painted a cheery yellow. Blue-and-white-checked curtains covered the knothole windows, through which slanted the early morning sunshine. Along the walls were rows and rows of cozy nests lined with warm flannel, each containing a sleeping orphan.

"There's Farthing, in the corner!" whispered Squeak. "Look, he's crept under the covers with Twist, the little angel."

"And there's Dodge—and Smudge from Scotland Yard!" said Glory.

The mice regarded the sleeping mouselings with satisfaction. "They'll be much better off here than on the streets," said Bubble. "A fine place, Nibbleswick."

The three of them tiptoed back downstairs again.

"Ah, there you are," said Sir Edmund. "And how are our young charges?"

"Out like little lights," reported Squeak.

"Visions of sugarplums dancing in their heads, no doubt," added Matron. She bustled across the carpet to a set of sliding doors and opened them. In the room beyond stood a long table heaped with food. A Christmas cracker lay across every plate. "Buckingham Palace sent over their very best," said Matron approvingly. "They always do, on Christmas."

Glory's stomach rumbled. She hadn't had much to eat

here in London so far. She sniffed the air expectantly. It smelled of wonderful things. Sugar and spice and evergreen. Just like Christmas.

"I'll light the tree, then, and we'll call the orphans to breakfast," said Matron.

She trundled back to the drawing room. A Christmas tree—the tip of a pine branch, actually—stood at the far end. It was covered with birthday candles. As Matron struck a match and lit each one, the bright strands of foraged ornaments and tinsel began to glitter and glow in the reflected light.

"Pretty!" cried a small voice behind them.

The mice turned to see Farthing standing on the carpet. He was sucking on his tail. On one side of him stood Twist, and on the other, Dodge.

"Happy Christmas, mouselings," said Sir Edmund.

The trio regarded him shyly.

"Santa Paws?" asked Farthing, staring wide-eyed at the elder mouse's silvered fur.

Sir Edmund chuckled. "Sorry to disappoint you," he said, shaking his head. "Though I did bring a few presents." He gestured toward the tree and the little ones scampered off.

Squeak leaned over to Glory. "Did I tell you my parents are planning to adopt Farthing?" she whispered.

"Hope you have plenty of mops back at the Savoy," said Glory with a smile, pointing to the puddle rippling out across the carpet beneath the excited mouseling.

"Oi! The little dickens nicked my watch," said Bubble

indignantly, patting his chest. Next to the tree, Twist swung the strap cheekily back and forth.

"He's got quick paws—you can say that much for him," said Sir Edmund, chuckling again. His laugh quickly turned to a harrumph as he realized his own watch and its silver chain were missing as well. He held out a stern paw. Twist sidled over to him and sheepishly placed the pilfered items in it.

"I'll be keeping a sharp eye on you," Sir Edmund warned him. He leaned closer and added with a twinkle, "If Matron here can steer your education in a more productive direction, we'll be recruiting you for spy school in a few years. You too," he said to Dodge. "Shame to let natural talent go to waste."

Dodge smiled and ducked her head.

"Oh, Glory, I almost forgot," said Squeak, pulling a small parcel out of her mitten-thumb backpack. "The doormouse at the Savoy passed this to me as we were leaving. It came by overnight courier with instructions to give it to you on Christmas morning."

Glory looked at the parcel curiously. *For Morning Glory Goldenleaf, the bravest mouse I know,* read the tag.

"Oh, my," she said. It was from Bunsen.

"Aren't you going to open it, Miss Glory?" asked Twist.

Dodge and Farthing crowded closer as she untied the ribbon and tore off the festive paper. Underneath was a small blue leather box tooled in gold.

"Pretty!" piped Farthing.

Glory opened the box. Inside, nestled in a scrap of matching blue velvet, was a tiny ring set with an exquisite diamond.

"Looks like someone has her own crown jewels," said Squeak, nudging Bubble.

Glory took the ring out of the box. Beneath it was a note in Bunsen's spiky scrawl. *Dear Glory, I love you with all my heart,* it said. *Will you marry me?*

"Oh, my," said Glory again, and turned a most Bunsen-like shade of pink.

Bubble and Squeak and the orphans looked at her expectantly. So did Sir Edmund and Matron. Glory slipped the ring over her paw. It fit perfectly.

"What are you going to tell him, Miss Glory? What's your answer?" Twist was bouncing up and down with excitement.

Glory smiled at the mouseling. Her eyes shone as bright as the diamond that adorned her paw. "It's the middle of the night back in America," she said firmly. "Bunsen will have to wait for his answer."

Matron herded the three orphans into the dining room and went to wake the others. As Bubble and Squeak and Sir Edmund took their places at the breakfast table, Glory gazed down at her paw. The engagement ring sparkled in the reflected firelight like the star on top of the Christmas tree.

"*Lux tenebras exstinguit,*" she whispered to herself, and went in to join her friends.